Shifting

SWANS LANDING #3

SHANA NORRIS

My bounty is as boundless as the sea,
My love as deep; the more I give to thee,
The more I have, for both are infinite.

- William Shakespeare, *Romeo and Juliet*

Chapter 1

One day I'd remember to do something with my hair before I went crabbing. I blew the lock of blonde hair that had fallen into my eyes out of the way, but it fell back down, blocking my vision once again. I eyed the stringy ends. Maybe I should cut it. I had never thought much about my hair, I let it grow and do what it wanted. But Josh Canavan had short hair, probably not even half an inch long. Was that what girls liked? Clean and neat?

Or more specifically, was that what Mara Westray liked?

I shook my head and bent back over the wooden dock that jutted into the Pamlico Sound. The sun, barely visible through the thick fog still lingering late in the day, sank over the water in front of me. I grabbed one of the thin, wet ropes dangling from the dock and pulled it out of the water.

"Yes!" I sat back on my feet, still squatting on the weathered dock, and opened the rusted wire box attached to the end of the rope. I dumped the one crab into a cracked bucket waiting nearby. The crab tumbled in on its back, flailed its legs a bit, and then managed to turn itself over. It scuttled around the empty container, claws snapping at the air.

"Sorry, buddy," I told the crab. "Looks like you'll be headed for the stove tonight." The crab waved a claw at me. "Don't look at me like that. You can thank my mom for it. She's the one who wanted crab."

I baited the crab pot with some raw chicken from the plastic bag tied to my belt loop and then tossed it back into the water. It didn't look like the crab dinner my mom wanted would go very far. One crab split among my parents, my little brother, and myself wouldn't give us each more than a bite. The three pots I'd already pulled up had all been empty.

I sighed, then moved down the dock toward the next pot. My lack of fishing success wasn't surprising. Every year the crab and fish population around the island decreased more and more. The strangely cold and foggy spring we were having didn't help get the sea life moving either.

As I reached for the next rope dangling from the edge of the dock, the crunch of footsteps on sand and broken shells beyond the tall grasses on the shore caught my attention.

"I said *no*," a girl's voice snapped. I glanced over my shoulder as two figures crested the small hill behind me. Dark hair whipped in the breeze, obscuring her face for a moment, but I had recognized the voice. Elizabeth

Connors. I could only assume the guy with her was one of her goon boyfriends. Kyle McCutcheon, it looked like. He seemed to be her guy of the week, judging from how she perched in his lap at lunch the other day. Not that I ever paid particular interest to Elizabeth and her group. She was hot, but she had made it her mission in life to make my best friend Sailor Mooring as miserable as possible, and that was something I couldn't forgive.

The stabbing ache still shot through me at the thought of Sailor. People always said time healed wounds, but it had been over two months since Sailor left and it hadn't gotten any easier yet.

"Liz," Kyle moaned, reaching for her. "Come *on.*" He almost sounded desperate. Whatever it was he wanted—and I could probably guess—Elizabeth obviously wasn't giving it up.

"Get off me, Kyle," she said as her feet slid over the sand.

It wasn't a private dock, so I couldn't tell them to leave, despite how much I wanted to. I hoped maybe I could stay invisible a while longer and they'd pass me by. I remained in my crouch, not daring to move. The water lapped at the sides of the dock. *Keep walking,* I chanted silently in tune with the slapping waves. *Just keep walking.*

Of course, I had never been lucky in my life and that wasn't about to change now.

Elizabeth saw me as she stepped onto the other end of the dock. She stopped abruptly, as confusion and then surprise passed across her face. Both emotions were replaced quickly with a smirk.

"Look, Kyle," she purred, reaching for him as if she hadn't just been fighting him off. "We have company."

Kyle looked over her head and spotted me. His face cracked into a stupid grin, making him look even dopier than usual. "Hey look, it's Nemo," he said, laughing at his own stupid joke.

I ignored them and reached for the rope to pull up the crab pot. I hadn't had many run-ins with Elizabeth and her crew since Sailor left. Sailor had always been Elizabeth's victim of choice, though she did go after Mara whenever she thought she could get away with it. But ever since Mara gave her a fat lip, Elizabeth had kept a low profile around us.

"Whatcha doing, Fish Boy?" Elizabeth asked. Her footsteps thumped down the dock toward me. "Looking for your cousins?"

"I ate them last week," Kyle said, letting out a loud burp.

I bit my tongue to keep back the crude response I wanted to say. I had always told Sailor to ignore them and they would go away. It had never worked, but fighting back never had either.

"Gross, Kyle," Elizabeth told him.

This pot held two crabs. I would have been thrilled with my catch if it hadn't been for Tweedledee and Tweedledum standing over me.

"So when's your little girlfriend coming home?" Elizabeth asked me. "Or did I run her off for good?"

I dumped the crabs into the bucket and then rebaited the pot before dropping it back into the water.

"Hey," Kyle said, kicking my leg with his toe. "She asked you a question."

I grabbed the bucket and scuttled like a crab over to the next line. It was the last one, at the very end of the dock. All I had to do was check this one and then I could go home.

Elizabeth and Kyle followed. "Shark got your tongue, Fish Boy?" she asked.

I reached down for the rope, clenching my teeth together as I kept my gaze on the water.

There was a movement next to me, and then my plastic bucket with the three crabs hurtled off the dock. It spun circles in the air before plummeting into the sound, dumping the crabs back into the water.

I spun around, glaring up at a grinning Kyle.

"Asshole!" I reached into the bag at my hip, grabbed a handful of raw chicken and hurled it at Kyle. It smacked him in the chest with a wet slurp.

Kyle lunged at me, but I stepped out of the way and he almost went off the end of the dock. He teetered on the edge, his arms waving wildly before he caught his balance.

"I'll kick your ass, Waverly," Kyle grunted.

Elizabeth stepped in front of him, pressing her hands against his chest. "Back off, Kyle."

His mouth hung open stupidly. "You're taking *his* side?"

"No, but you kind of asked for it," she said. She gave me a withering look. "Let's just go. It's starting to smell rotten around here."

Kyle glared at me, but he followed Elizabeth. As they walked back down the dock, I leaned down, pulling the bucket from the water. It was empty and my catch was gone. Great. Mom would be thrilled when I came home empty-handed.

Or maybe not empty-handed. I had one last pot left.

"Kyle, *stop*," Elizabeth's voice floated back to me. They were still on the dock, halfway back to the shore. Kyle stepped closer to her, his hands pawing over her waist. "Come on," he said. "You know you want to."

Charming. No wonder girls fell all over the idiot.

I pulled the pot toward the surface, grinning when I found two crabs inside. At least Mom could have crab for dinner. The rest of us would eat hot dogs or something.

"I said get off of me!" Elizabeth said, her tone sounding more irritated.

"I'll be quick," Kyle said, his voice muffled as he pressed his face into her shoulder.

It's not my problem, I told myself as I shook the crabs from the pot and into my bucket. *I don't care. It doesn't concern*—

"Ow! Kyle, stop!" Elizabeth's shout echoed back to me, the worried tone in her voice making the hairs on my neck prickle. "I mean it!"

Oh, hell.

"Leave her alone," I said as I walked down the dock toward them. Both Elizabeth and Kyle turned toward me, their eyes wide with surprise.

"Go back to your crabs," Kyle growled.

"Actually, I'm all done," I said, swinging the bucket with the two crabs back and forth as evidence. "So if you would get out of here and leave her alone, I'll be on my way."

Kyle stepped away from Elizabeth and toward me, his teeth clenched and nostrils flaring. "This isn't your business, shark bait." He fluttered his fingers at me. "Swim off back to your sandcastle."

He reached toward Elizabeth, his thick fingers closing around her wrist. "Come on, Liz. Let's go somewhere a little more private."

Elizabeth pulled herself free from his grasp. "Go away, Kyle."

Kyle looked at her like she'd lost her mind. "You'd rather stay here with this loser?" he asked, gesturing toward me.

"No," Elizabeth said. "But I'm bored with you." She yawned wide as emphasis.

Kyle didn't make any movement to leave. He stared at her, confusion etched across his dopey features.

"You heard her." I should have left and let them sort this all out themselves, but I had already gotten myself into it. The guy may have been a neanderthal, but he was also much bigger than Elizabeth. I didn't want that on my conscience when I tried to go to sleep later. "Why don't you run along back to your shack?"

Kyle's lips curled into a sneer. "You think you're gonna make me, Waverly?" He puffed up his chest like the roosters in Mrs. Sampson's front yard getting ready to fight. "I ain't scared of no little fish—"

As Kyle spoke the last word, I swung my bucket of crabs at his head. The two crabs inside came flying out, falling onto Kyle's shoulder. Surprised, he stepped back, dancing a little jig as he brushed the crabs off. One foot went backward again and then *splash*.

Kyle came up sputtering next to the dock, his perfectly combed hair now soaked and sticking to his head.

I snatched up the crabs from the dock before they could escape back into the sound and returned them to the bucket. Then I leaned down toward where Kyle was trying to get his footing on the soft sand.

"You keep forgetting one thing, McCutcheon. I ain't no fish." I looked back at Elizabeth. "I'm leaving. Either you go too, or you stay behind with this creep. It's up to you."

Elizabeth's gaze darted between me and Kyle, who slipped and crashed back into the water again. She shot me a smirk before sauntering down the dock, tossing her hair over her shoulder.

I spit into the water near where Kyle glared up at me, gave him a big grin, and then followed Elizabeth down the dock, swinging my crab bucket from one finger.

Chapter 2

"It's been almost two months, Dylan," Mara said as I stepped to her side later that evening on the empty strip of beach known as Pirate's Cove. Her gaze never left the ocean stretched before us, the foamy waves crashing against the shore endlessly . She wrapped her arms around herself in a tight hug. Black wisps had fallen out of her messy bun and now whipped around her head as a breeze swept over the Atlantic Ocean.

I stared out at a place in the distance where the ocean blended into the gray sky. The chill in the air made it feel like we were still stuck in late winter even though it was now May.

"It's a long swim," I told her.

Mara sighed, the sound almost matching the song of the water that vibrated through me and mixed with the energy of the earth beneath my bare feet.

"I feel like I should have heard something," she said. "Or *feel* something. I should know if he's still alive, right?"

I clenched my teeth together, fighting back the grimace that thoughts of Josh Canavan caused. Even though he had been gone since mid-March, his presence was still very much alive here on the island.

"Maybe you don't feel anything because he *is* alive. Maybe you'd only feel something if he were..." I couldn't say the word. No matter how I felt about Josh, I had to believe he was still alive out there somewhere. That he was finding his way toward the ancestral home of our people and would eventually come back to Swans Landing.

As long as Josh was okay, I could believe Sailor was alive too.

Mara turned her gaze away from the water, her golden brown eyes studying me for a moment. "Do *you* think they're still out there?" she asked.

Blonde hair whipped across my face for a moment, before the wind whipped it back the other way.

"Yes. They're still alive."

I didn't want to think about Josh and Sailor, or a place none of us on the island had ever seen. The ancient homeland, if it even existed at all, was nothing more than a myth to us. Whatever was going on out there didn't change anything here.

I had to focus on the now. Mara and I were still here, and I hated that she spent her time outside of school standing on this beach, waiting for someone who might never return.

"Come on," I said, unbuttoning my cut-off khaki

shorts. "Let's go for a swim."

I didn't wait for her answer. I kicked out of my clothes, shivering a little in the weak sun that barely filtered through the haze as I splashed into the water. It was cold, but I was finfolk, and I was born to survive the ocean.

"Dylan!" Mara's shout reached me over the water, but I forged farther into the waves, feeling the shudders beginning deep in my bones as the change took hold of me. I dipped under the surface, immersing myself in the salt water and filling my belly with a huge gulp of it. I twisted and bucked under the water as my body reformed itself, legs becoming one long blue-scaled tail.

When it was done, I propelled myself toward the surface and leaped into the air, arms stretched out in front of me as I arced back into the ocean.

I surfaced again and shook my head, clearing water from my eyes as I looked back toward shore. The beach was empty.

Another head popped up from the waves near me, spraying water from her mouth. Mara's hair clung to her brown skin, rivulets of water running down her cheeks and dripping from her chin. I eyed the neckline of her T-shirt, now soaked and clinging to her body. When the water dipped low enough, I could see the shape of her breasts beneath the cloth and I couldn't keep my gaze from straying to that area.

"Good day for a swim," I said.

Mara laughed. I liked her laugh. "You think every day is a good day for a swim."

I shrugged. "I am finfolk."

She leaned back and flicked her golden tail fin,

splashing water in my direction. She was becoming better at swimming and controlling her finfolk form. She looked natural in the water, as if she had spent her whole life swimming it.

I wanted that ease, that confidence she had. It was what had drawn me to her the day we first met.

I still wanted her to choose me, even though she belonged to someone else.

I pushed these thoughts away and focused on the now. I had these moments alone with her. She may have been waiting for Josh to come back, but for now, I had her to myself.

I grabbed her hand, letting my tail fin sweep across hers under the water. Mara looked at me, her eyebrows raised. I could see the objection in her face. She opened her mouth and I could already hear the "let's just be friends" speech starting in her mind.

Before she could say anything, I said, "Come on, let's swim." And then I dove under the water, pulling her with me.

Chapter 3

Propping the old broom against my shoulder, I checked over the rough wood floor of Moody's Variety Store for any tracks of sand I had missed. The shop was old and dusty, so my attempts at sweeping didn't amount to much of a difference.

"Looks good," Jim Moody, the owner of Swans Landing's only grocery store/video rental/bookstore grunted from his place behind the counter. He nodded to some empty boxes along one wall. "Take those out back and break them down. Put them with the others. You'll see them when you get out there."

"Yes, sir," I said as I bent to retrieve the stack.

I had only recently taken on work at Moody's. My parents weren't exactly thrilled about it, since I was already working with Lake most mornings.

"You should be focusing on school," my mom always

said. "You take on too much responsibility doing other things."

"What's the point?" I would ask. She would only give me that look, the one that said "I'm the parent and I know best." But even she couldn't deny that I would never leave the island to go off to college. Finfolk didn't do that. Some had tried, but they always came back. We couldn't go farther inland without feeling the effects of being too far from the ocean. There wasn't a college in Swans Landing, or anywhere else along North Carolina's Outer Banks, so my options were pretty much limited to remaining here. The ones in coastal cities weren't close enough to the ocean to keep my body satisfied.

No, my future was already set in the vibrations of the water and earth here on the island. I'd most likely become a fisherman or else make trinkets for the declining tourist industry. Either way, focusing on high school didn't seem to be important.

Most human business owners in Swans Landing didn't hire finfolk, so I was lucky to get this job. But then, Mr. Moody wasn't exactly like most other humans.

The day was cool and cloudy and the wind whipped my jacket around my body as I descended the wooden staircase outside Moody's. The shop sat on top of wooden pilings, raised off the ground in case of floods from hurricanes, like most other homes and buildings on the island.

I went around back and began stomping the boxes flat. I could see exactly where Mr. Moody wanted them to go, since there was already a huge pile of boxes back there, most of them water-stained and soggy. He didn't seem to consider actually getting rid of the boxes to be much of a priority.

I was so focused on stomping the boxes I didn't hear the crunch of gravel and sand to warn me that I wasn't alone. The sound of a voice made me jump.

"Hello, Fish Boy."

I whipped around to find Elizabeth Connors standing only a few feet away, her arms crossed over her chest. She wore low cut sweater and my gaze immediately strayed to the deep vee of the collar, where the crossing of her arms accentuated her cleavage. She may have been a bitch, but she was still hot.

"What do you want?" I asked, resuming my task of flattening boxes.

"I was out for a walk and saw you coming down the stairs." She stepped toward me, keeping her arms crossed tight and swinging her hips a little. "I heard you're working here now."

"Yeah," I said. "Mr. Moody offered me Sailor's old job." Not that Sailor ever really worked at Moody's. She was technically employed there, but she rarely showed up to work. She never seemed comfortable around Mr. Moody, even though he was her grandfather. But then, Mr. Moody never seemed comfortable around her either.

Elizabeth wrinkled her nose. I wasn't sure if it was at the mention of Sailor, or the fact that I was working.

I went back to crushing the boxes, but Elizabeth didn't move. I felt her standing there, her green eyes watching me.

"Did you need something?" I finally asked, when her staring started to get on my nerves. It made my skin prickle, the way she just watched as I stomped the boxes.

"I had a question I wanted to ask." She tilted her head

to one side.

"What?"

"How do..." She grinned, a wicked gleam in her eye. "How do you people...*you know*?"

I shook my head. "No, I don't know. I have no idea what you're talking about."

"I was wondering, how much of you is fish and how much is human?" She stood with one hip jutted out, the wind whipping her brown hair across her face.

I scowled. "None of me is fish."

"So then," she started, her gaze flitting down toward the front of my jeans, "you have all the normal parts?"

Immediately, it dawned on me what exactly she was asking. A hot flush creeped up my neck and I glared at her, clenching my teeth together. I scanned the area, looking for Jackie or Elizabeth's other little groupies that followed her around. We were alone, but that didn't make me relax.

"If this is one of your dumb jokes, I'm not in the mood." I grabbed the rest of the crushed boxes and flung them into the pile under the shop. Then I stomped toward the stairs, brushing past her.

"Wait." Elizabeth hurried to block my path, pressing her hand flat against my chest. Her skin felt warm, even through the cotton of my shirt. Elizabeth Connors had *never* touched me before. She avoided any contact with finfolk as much as possible. In second grade, we'd taken a school field trip to the Cape Hatteras Lighthouse, and Elizabeth and I had been assigned class buddies. We were supposed to hold hands as we walked to keep from getting lost, but Elizabeth had refused to touch me, claiming I would be "slimy like a fish." For as long as I'd known her, Elizabeth had followed along with her father's insults against us.

Elizabeth's slender fingers rested on my chest. She didn't move her hand. We stood only inches apart under the shadow of the back stairs leading up to Moody's, Elizabeth's face tilted up toward mine.

"Why did you help me the other night?" she asked in a low voice.

I swallowed. "Kyle was being a jerk. Anyone would have done the same thing."

She shook her head. "No, they wouldn't. We had just left a whole group of people and none of them tried to stop Kyle when I told him not to touch me."

"Maybe you should get new friends," I told her.

Her eyes were hooded as she looked up at me, her mouth curled into a small smile at the corners. Her hand was still on my chest, sending a tingling sensation radiating outward. She smelled like floral perfume, so different from the smell of salt and sand that permeated Swans Landing. "You're different from other guys. Special. Unique."

"I'm a regular guy." I hoped she couldn't feel the way my heart had suddenly started beating overtime under her hand.

Elizabeth shook her head. "You're not, Dylan Waverly. You never have been a regular guy." She stepped closer to me and the smell of her perfume made me feel a little light-headed.

I licked my lips, which had gone dry. "What do you want, Elizabeth?" I asked again.

"To figure something out," she whispered.

She bridged the space between us, raising herself on

tiptoe. Her face moved closer, a small fraction of an inch as each second passed until finally, her lips pressed against mine.

She was soft and warm and the smell of her perfume seemed to wrap around us. My hands moved on their own, resting on the curve of her hips, steadying her as she leaned into me. Her hand on my chest moved upward until her fingers threaded through the ponytail at the back of my neck while her other hand slipped around my waist, pressing against my back.

Before this moment, I had kissed two girls in my life. But Sailor and Mara were both finfolk. I had never kissed a human girl before. She tasted earthy, not like the salty tinge of a finfolk kiss. Her kiss made me think of sunshine on meadows, open fields of earth I had never seen except in pictures.

"Hmm," Elizabeth said as she stepped back, breaking the kiss.

My mind reeled with the effects of her kiss. It took every bit of restraint I had not to pull her to me again. I wanted that closeness, the feel of someone next to me, the touch of her skin against mine. I wanted earth and sky and sun.

"What?" I asked, my voice cracking.

"You taste like the ocean, Fish Boy." She ran her fingers through my ponytail again, tugging on the ends of my hair. "See you around."

I was unable to do anything except watch as she stepped out from under the stairs, walking back toward the road in front of Moody's, her hips swaying casually as if nothing out of the ordinary had happened.

The only thing I could do was stare after her and think, *What the hell was that?*

Chapter 4

"So how was school?" Mom asked, smiling at my younger brother Reed and me across the table.

I shrugged. "Fine. Same as usual."

"Soccer practice," Reed said, as if this explained his whole day. For my twelve-year-old brother, soccer was practically his whole life. He tried much harder to fit in among the humans of Swans Landing than I did, though it didn't always work. I had never taken an interest in land sports and Swans Landing School didn't have a swim team. I would have been great on a swim team, though I had an unfair advantage.

Mom looked at my dad, raising her eyebrows. "And you? How was your day? Any more exciting?"

Dad chewed a bite of roasted potato and swallowed before answering. "Same as usual," he said.

Mom rolled her eyes and sighed. "Men. It doesn't

matter if they're finfolk or human, they still aren't proficient at verbal communication." She wiped her mouth and then said, "Well, my day was interesting. Harry Connors was in the office."

I tried not to look too interested as my stomach clenched at the mention of Elizabeth's father. Had he found out about his daughter kissing me earlier that afternoon? Even though Mara had saved Mr. Connors from drowning, he still hadn't changed his mind about finfolk.

My dad's lip curled slightly. "What did he want?"

Mom worked as a secretary for Kinsey Attorney at Law, which was the only law firm on the island. Her boss, Mona Kinsey, wasn't finfolk, but she didn't have any ill will toward us. She was one the few humans on the island who didn't mind living alongside finfolk.

"The usual," Mom said, sighing. "He came to talk to Mrs. Kinsey about filing suit against Lake for tampering with his crab pots."

"Lake isn't doing that!" I protested. "Mr. Connors is the one invading Lake's territory. He's destroyed some of Lake's pots. Lake should sue *him*."

Mom raised her eyebrows. "Does Lake have any proof that it was Mr. Connors who did this?"

I sank back in my chair, shaking my head. "No."

Mom gave me a sympathetic smile. "That's the issue. Both sides can blame each other all they want, but without evidence we don't have a case against either one."

"Did Mrs. Kinsey tell him that?" Dad asked.

"Yes," Mom said, "though I don't know what good it will do. Harry is holding a grudge, and he won't be happy until he does something." Her forehead creased in little lines. "I have a feeling this won't go away. Harry has been getting angrier lately, like he's determined to prove something." She sighed heavily. "I think something bad is going to happen."

I set my fork down on my plate and studied her. "You think Mr. Connors will do something to Lake?"

She tried to give me a reassuring smile, but it didn't quite meet her eyes. "I don't know, honey. It's probably nothing. It's this strange weather we're having. I think it has set everyone on edge."

"We've lived on this island together for years," Dad added. "We should be able to keep coexisting as we always have."

I returned my mom's smile, to make her think I wasn't worried. But I knew she wasn't telling the truth. Because the truth was, what we had been doing for the last sixteen years wasn't coexisting the way we always had. When Josh's father had an affair with Sailor's mother and then drowned one night while the finfolk were in the water, it changed the way humans and finfolk interacted. Maybe if we knew what had really happened that night, we could move on.

But it was a sixteen-year-old mystery, and it didn't look like anyone would come forward now with the truth.

Sailor, I thought, *if you're out there, you need to find your mother and come home quick.* Coral Mooring, wherever she was, may have been the only person who might know what happened that night. If she was still alive.

* * *

"What exactly is this?" Mara spooned up a glob of something gray from her lunch tray and then let it plop back down into the rest of the unappetizing mass of congealed food.

"I think it's gravy," said her friend Claire.

My gaze roamed over their shoulders, to the table across the room where Elizabeth Connors sat with her friends. She faced me, but she had avoided looking my way ever since I'd entered the cafeteria. I'd walked right by her table on my way from the lunch line and still Elizabeth didn't look up. Like I didn't exist. Like she hadn't kissed me behind Moody's the day before.

"Does this look like gravy to you?" Mara shoved the spoonful of gray quivering glob in front of my face.

I leaned back, wrinkling my nose. "No, that's why I didn't get it." I gestured to my chicken salad sandwich and bag of chips.

"I'm tired of sandwiches," Mara said, plopping the glob back into her tray. "That's all I eat at Lake's house. That's all he knows how to cook."

"Miss Gale will bring you some food," I said, shrugging.

Mara's jaw twitched and a line formed between her eyebrows. "Miss Gale hasn't exactly been in a cooking mood lately."

Why hadn't I thought about that before I spoke? Miss Gale was usually happy and lively, but ever since Sailor left, she'd been kind of depressed. She didn't talk much, she didn't even leave her house very often. She used to work a few days a week at Moody's, but I'd noticed she was coming in less often. When was the last time I'd

23

seen her? Maybe a week?

I made a mental note to go by and check on her soon. Miss Gale was like a grandmother to me and I hated to think of her sitting alone in her house.

My gaze wandered over to Elizabeth's table again. She was sitting next to a guy in our class, Gabe. Kyle sat at the other end of the table, sending glares their way. As I watched, Elizabeth laughed and then leaned over to bump her shoulder against Gabe's. I gritted my teeth together, my eyes narrowing.

"Yoohoo, Dylan!" Mara waved at me, scowling a little.

I blinked. Mara and Claire gave me the same confused look. "What?" I asked.

"Are you okay?" Mara asked, furrowing her brow as she studied me. "You seem a little out of it today."

I bent over my tray and tore my sandwich in half, stuffing one piece in my mouth all at once. "I'm fine," I said through a mouthful of sandwich.

Mara didn't look like she believed me, but she didn't press further. "Claire and I are going to the lighthouse this afternoon to take some pictures," she said. "You want to come?"

I didn't have anything planned for the afternoon. I wasn't working at Moody's that day, and Lake had said he didn't need me that afternoon. So I was free to do whatever I wanted.

My gaze flicked back to Elizabeth, who was now whispering in her friend Jackie's ear. My stomach twisted. Was she telling Jackie what had happened between us? A part of me still believed it was all a joke, something Elizabeth had done so she could laugh about it with her friends later. Like, let's see how far we can push Fish Boy before he explodes.

But when they broke apart, neither of them glanced my way. Jackie didn't seem extremely shocked or anything out of the ordinary. But if Elizabeth hadn't told her what had happened, what exactly did that mean it was?

"Dylan?" Mara asked, raising her eyebrows.

"Um," I said, "no, I...I have something I have to do."

Mara shrugged. "Okay." She turned back to Claire and they talked about some pictures Mara wanted to take.

I didn't know why I hadn't told Mara about Elizabeth's kiss. If I talked about it, would I realize it had all been a hallucination?

But it had felt real. And it had felt good.

Across the room, Elizabeth stood up from her table. Jackie started to stand too, but then Elizabeth said something to her and Jackie sat back down. I watched as Elizabeth walked over to the trash cans, dumping the remains of her lunch, and then headed across the room toward the door. My heart raced into overtime. She would have to walk right by me to leave. She'd have to acknowledge my presence, at least look at me as she passed.

But she kept her gaze focused on the door behind me as she drew closer. My hands gripped the edge of the table and I didn't dare breathe as she continued across the room. A roaring sound had filled my ears so I couldn't hear any of the conversations around me.

Just as I thought she'd ignore me completely as she passed, Elizabeth's eyes flicked my way. She raised one

25

eyebrow, the corners of her lips curling slightly, as if in a dare. A dare to do what—follow her? Kiss her in front of everyone? Or let her keep going, playing this game that there was nothing going on between us?

As Elizabeth stepped through the doors of the cafeteria, I pushed my chair back with a sudden screech. Claire and Mara broke off in mid-conversation to look at me as I stood quickly.

"I have to go," I said, grabbing my backpack. "To the library. I forgot. See you later."

The words tumbled out as I turned, almost tripping over my chair leg. I hurried down the corridor away from the cafeteria. Elizabeth walked a few feet ahead, her hips swaying. She didn't look back, and I wasn't sure if it was because she knew I'd follow or because she didn't care.

She turned a corner, then another, leading me farther away from my friends and everyone else in our normal lives. At last, she slipped into an empty classroom, leaving the door partially open behind her.

I paused in the doorway, peeking into the room. Elizabeth sat on a desk in the back of the room, away from the windows. I slipped inside, shutting the door behind me.

"Well," she said, looking at me as I stood in place, "what do you want?"

I couldn't answer that question. I didn't know why I had followed her, except that I was unable to stop myself.

"I'm not comfortable with long silences, Fish Boy," she said, rolling her eyes.

It was that name, Fish Boy, that made me move. I

dropped my bag on the floor and closed the distance between us, maneuvering myself in between her knees. She leaned back on the palms of her hands, looking up at me as her hair fell away from her face like a dark waterfall.

Her lips were pink and full. I tried to stop my hand from shaking as I reached around the back of her neck, cradling her head in my fingers. Then I leaned down and pressed my lips to hers, absorbing that earthy taste of faraway places once again.

Chapter 5

The distinct sound of a door closing and footsteps moving across the tiled kitchen floor broke through the fog that had invaded my brain.

"You have to go." I sat up and reached for my T-shirt, which had been tossed onto the floor in a crumpled heap fifteen minutes before. I pulled it on, forcing myself not to think about what might have happened, could have happened if my brother hadn't come home.

Elizabeth rolled across my bed toward me, still fully dressed, though the clothes hadn't stopped me from exploring the curves underneath. She slipped her hand under the hem of my shirt, pressing her warm palm against my back.

"Do you really want me to go?" she asked in that low, purring tone that made my pulse race.

I didn't want her to leave. It was the last thing I wanted. I wanted her pressed against me again, my hands on her skin. I wanted her lips on mine. I wanted more.

But I could hear the sounds of Reed rummaging for a snack down the hall. "My brother is home," I said. "You have to go."

Elizabeth sat up, her hair wild and messed up in just the right way. The way that made me think of touching her again. I stood and moved toward the mirror over my dresser, trying to press the top of my hair back down.

I could see Elizabeth pouting at me in the mirror's reflection. "You're a tease, Dylan Waverly."

"I didn't ask you to come here, you know." I pulled my hair back, grabbing a rubber band from my dresser and twisting it quickly around the ragged ponytail.

Elizabeth shrugged and then slid from my bed. The bottom of her shorts rode high on her thighs, revealing white skin I couldn't help staring at. "Fine. Maybe I won't come back."

I scowled at her, tearing my eyes away from her thighs. "Fine. What is this anyway? Some random hook up? Something to laugh about with your friends?"

Her eyes flashed as she returned my scowl. "My friends can *never* know about this. No one can. Got that?"

"Afraid they'd start tormenting you as much as you've tormented us all these years?"

She wrinkled her nose, crossing her arms. "Like anyone would believe you over me. If you say anything about this to anyone, I'll deny it ever happened. I'll make you sorry you were born."

"I'm sure Kyle and his idiot friends would be more

than happy to pummel me in order to protect your honor." I leaned against the dresser, smirking. "Don't worry. Your dirty little secret is safe. Do you know what Mara would do to me if she found out about this? Or Sailor?"

"Well," Elizabeth said, tossing her hair over her shoulder, "I don't have to worry about Sailor, do I? She's long gone."

I clenched my teeth. "She's coming back."

"If she didn't get eaten by a shark."

I glared at her and then stalked across the room, pushing open the window. "Get out," I said.

Elizabeth sneered. "I'm not climbing out your window."

"There's a wraparound porch, you'll be fine. Go around to the staircase and you can disappear back to your perfect life. No one will know." I raised my eyebrows at her. "Unless you'd like to walk out the front door and explain to my brother why you're here. He's not very good at keeping secrets, by the way."

Elizabeth shot me a withering look, but she climbed onto the window sill. She paused, one leg outside and the other still inside, then leaned over and kissed me once again. "It was fun, Fish Boy. Hope to do it again."

With that, she slipped out of my room. I heard her footsteps thump across the wooden deck as she headed toward the stairs leading to the backyard. A memory of another girl slipping out that window flashed through my mind. Not that long ago, Mara had sneaked out of my room just like this after spending the night with me.

Two girls in my bed within the space of two months and yet I still hadn't managed to score more than a few kisses and gropings.

I felt like I needed a cold shower, but I'd settle for a cold bowl of ice cream.

Reed sat at the kitchen table, dunking cookies into a tall glass of milk. "Did I see someone on the deck?" he asked.

I buried my head in the freezer as I searched for my mom's homemade ice cream. She always added more salt than the recipe actually called for, which made it perfect for finfolk tastes. "I have no idea what you're talking about," I told him.

"I could have sworn I saw someone running down the stairs. Someone who looked like a girl." Reed gave me a sly grin, his teeth coated with black chunks of cookie.

"No girls here." I grabbed a bowl and plunked two generous spoonfuls of ice cream into it, then headed over to the table. "What would a girl be doing here anyway?"

Reed raised his eyebrows. "Do we need to have the talk about the birds and the bees? Or in our case, the jellyfish and the dolphins?"

I flicked a piece of ice cream across the table. It hit him in the center of his forehead.

"Hey!" Reed wiped the ice cream away with the back of his hand, then licked it off.

I bent over my bowl, eating slowly. Whenever I brought my hand near my face for another spoonful, I could smell the faint scent of Elizabeth's perfume on my skin. I breathed it in, remembering how soft and warm she had been.

"It's cool, you know," Reed said. "I mean, if you do

have a girlfriend hiding out in your room. I won't tell Mom and Dad." He looked hopeful, like maybe he wanted me to tell him about my secret love life so he could live vicariously through me.

But what would I tell? I didn't even know what all of this was.

"No," I said in a flat tone. "No girlfriends. Sorry, kid."

* * *

"Miss Gale?" I opened the door slowly, dropping my keys back into my pocket. Sailor had given me a key to her house long ago, as a backup in case she ever lost hers. That had never happened, and so my key hadn't been used until now.

I didn't normally walk into other people's houses uninvited, but I'd been knocking for ten minutes and Miss Gale still hadn't come to the door. I couldn't stop the gnawing feeling in my stomach, like something was trying to eat its way out. Miss Gale hadn't shown up for work at Moody's that day. When I'd asked Mr. Moody about it, he had shrugged and said she wasn't feeling well.

Miss Gale didn't get sick. She'd never taken a day off in all the years I'd known her.

The house was dark, the curtains pulled shut over the windows. The only light came from the skylights overhead, where dozens of crystal prisms hung from fishing line. Sailor and I had helped Miss Gale put those up one summer when we were seven. I still liked the way the rainbow light flashed along the blue walls. Being in

Miss Gale's house almost felt like being underwater. My footsteps echoed through the silent house. The air conditioner was running high, and my skin prickled in the cold air. "Miss Gale? It's Dylan. Are you home?"

Like most other people on the island, Miss Gale didn't own a car, so I couldn't check the driveway for indication of whether she was home or not. But I didn't think she'd be anywhere else, since Mara had said Miss Gale was spending a lot of time at home lately.

The floorboards creaked as I walked down the hall. "Miss Gale?" I knocked softly on her door. "Can I come in?"

I thought I heard a noise inside, though I couldn't make out a word. I pushed the door open carefully, peering in at the big bed across the room.

The only times I had ever been in Miss Gale's room were when I was a kid and Sailor would convince me to go along with one of her plans, which usually involved getting into something of Miss Gale's that she didn't want us to touch—her expensive face cream or old letters—and always ended with the two of us getting into trouble. I couldn't even remember how many times Miss Gale had threatened to whip my behind, though she never actually did it.

The room hadn't changed much from what I remembered. I took in a quick glance at the old wooden furniture, the dresser filled with dozens of framed photographs, and a plush blue chair in front of the tall window, then I walked over to the bed, where I could see Miss Gale's shape under the covers.

Her eyes were opened halfway, but she looked pale and her gaze unfocused. Her lips were a light pink, her long white hair loosened from its usual braid and her breathing slow and ragged.

"Miss Gale." I sat down on the edge of the bed, reaching over to smooth back a lock of hair from her cheek. She felt cold, and if it weren't for the steady sound of her breathing, I would have almost thought she was... I gulped, pushing away the thought.

"Are you okay?" I asked. "Are you sick?"

Miss Gale's eyes fluttered open the rest of the way and she looked at me, searching my face for a moment. "Dylan," she rasped. "Is Sailor..." Her voice trailed off, even though her lips moved.

"Sailor isn't back yet," I told her gently. When Miss Gale's mouth curved into a deeper frown, I added, "But she should be back soon. She can't stay gone forever."

I didn't know if my words were the truth or not. Sailor's mother had never come back, neither had any other finfolk who had left Swans Landing over the years. One by one, they had all disappeared, and no one came back despite the songs we sang each month on the night of the new moon.

But this was Sailor Mooring. If anyone could come back, it would be her.

Miss Gale swallowed, an action that seemed to take a lot of effort. I frowned and asked, "Have you had anything to drink lately?" I looked around for a glass or a bottle or some evidence that Miss Gale had been drinking—or even eating—but there was none.

"I'll be right back," I told her.

I hurried to the kitchen and filled a tall glass with water. Then I pried open the salt shaker and dumped half of the canister into the glass. I stirred the water as I walked back to Miss Gale's room.

"Drink." I helped her to move into a sitting position and then held the glass while Miss Gale drank.

When she had taken several large gulps, she leaned her head back, sighing. Already, her skin looked better, closer to her normal color. Her eyes were brighter and more focused.

"What's wrong?" I asked. "Do you need to see a doctor?"

Miss Gale closed her eyes and shook her head. "Doctors can't help our kind, Dylan, you know that. Ever since Sailor left, something hasn't felt right. It's like when her mama left all those years ago. Except this time I'm too old to fight back."

I reached for Miss Gale's hand and squeezed. "I miss her too. She'll be back soon, I know it."

Miss Gale frowned. "No, it's not just that. I do miss her, but there's something *else*. Something...I don't know. Something *missing*. Something that was here but is now gone. It's not just Sailor. I've felt it in the past, when others have left the island." She looked at me intently. "Don't you feel it?"

I shook my head. "I don't know what you mean."

Miss Gale sighed. "Maybe it's because you're young. You're stronger. But us older folk, we can feel it. Something changes on the island every time a finfolk leaves."

"Like the song?" I asked. Every time a finfolk disappeared, it was heard in our singing on Song Night. The song was never as strong as it had been before and the voices didn't blend as they once had.

"Maybe," Miss Gale said. She shook her head again.

"I'm not sure exactly what I mean."

She looked so tired and frail, something I had never seen Miss Gale look before. "Do you need anything?" I asked her. "I'll stay with you if you want, until Sailor comes back. I'm sure my parents will understand."

Miss Gale smiled up at me and patted my hand. "No, thank you, Dylan. Jim comes by to check on me every so often, and Mara and Lake come. I'll be fine." She reached up to tug at my hair. "You're such a sweet boy. But you do need a hair cut."

I laughed. "You always say that."

"And you never listen," she said. "You and Lake both. But I reckon y'all wouldn't be right any other way."

I fluffed up the sides of her pillow and tucked her blanket around her. I didn't know if she wanted to be tucked in, but it was what my mom had always done for me when I was sick. It was comforting, at least I hoped it was.

"Sailor loves you," Miss Gale told me as I stood. "So I know she'll be back, because she wouldn't leave you for good."

I wasn't so sure about that. We'd had a fight the day before she left and I had said some things to her that I wished I could take back.

"I always imagined you two getting married one day," she went on, smiling as she closed her eyes. "I'd be happy to have you as my grandson-in-law."

My stomach churned as memories of kissing Elizabeth flooded my mind. I had kissed Sailor once, years ago when we both wanted to get our first kiss over with. But kissing her had never felt the way it did when I kissed Elizabeth. How terrible of a person did that make me, that I couldn't even feel the same way about the most important person in my life as I did about the person I had always hated?

"I'll come back tomorrow to check on you," I said softly as I walked out of the room, leaving Miss Gale's comment unanswered.

Chapter 6

Mara blinked up at the gray sky, nodding approvingly at the clouds overhead. "Perfect," she stated, pulling her camera from around her neck and turning a few dials.

The wind whipped my hair around my head and I pushed it back with one hand. "Are you sure?" It didn't look like a perfect day. A storm threatened on the horizon and the clouds looked fat with rain. The ocean crashed against the pilings of the broken pier. We stood under the structure where it rose up from the wet sand. I glanced up at the rotting wood over my head, hoping the rest of the pier wouldn't crash down on me.

"I'm sure," Mara said confidently. She adjusted a dial on her camera again, then held it up so she could see the LCD screen on the back. She clicked the button a couple of times, taking a few test shots. I didn't know a lot about photography, but I'd been around her enough lately to know that she never started a photo shoot without testing her exposures first.

Honestly, I wasn't excited to be Mara's model for the day. If Josh had been here, I was sure she would have asked him to pose for pictures by the pier and not me. I tried not to let it bother me that I was her default choice since Josh was gone. I should have been happy she'd asked me at all. I *liked* spending time with Mara. I wanted to spend as much time alone with her as I could.

But I felt the weight of my cell phone in my pocket, waiting for a text that hadn't yet come.

"What do you want me to do?" I asked.

Mara backed up a few steps. "Act natural. Stand there and look at the water. Walk. Whatever you want. I want to play with textures."

I shoved my hands into the pockets of my cut-off khakis. The wind whipped my hair into my mouth as Mara started clicking away with her camera. I felt ridiculous.

"What do you mean, textures?" I asked.

"I mean the way the lines of your clothes and hair and skin contrast against the roughness of the wooden pilings and the foaming water." Mara knelt, not seeming to notice that her knees would be soaked from the wet sand.

I still didn't know exactly what she meant, but I decided not to question her further. Mara took beautiful photographs. She had a way of capturing life with her camera, like her dad could capture it within his seashell artwork. I wasn't exactly artistic. Stringing shells on fishing line didn't count as works of art and didn't take much skill.

I kicked off my shoes and pressed my toes into the wet sand. On the edge of where the ocean met the beach, I could feel the call of both water and earth within me. Part of me wanted to dive in and swim, while the other part wanted to stay rooted to the land. It was hard to fight these two opposing sides of myself. Sometimes it would be easier if I was fully human, if I could walk around every day like the people at school, ignoring the water if I chose to, able to go and do whatever I wanted.

Instead, I was tied here, stuck to live out my life on this island, caught between land and water.

"What was it like before you came here?" I asked, casting a glance over my shoulder at Mara. "When you lived in Memphis, I mean? What was it like to not live near the ocean?"

Mara shrugged as she continued to take photos. "I don't know. It was just normal. It was what I'd always known."

"Didn't it hurt be so far from the water?"

"Not really," Mara said. "In the back of my mind, I always knew something was missing, but I didn't know what. I had never changed form before, so I don't think the ocean had the hold on me that it does now." She frowned. "I guess now I can't go too far from the water, can I?"

I shook my head as the water slipped across the sand, foaming around my toes. It called to me, begging me to go in and swim. "You'll feel like you're drowning on air if you try to leave the ocean. The earth's essence can sustain you for a short time, but the water will always call you back."

"How far inland have you gone?" Mara asked.

"I used to go see a doctor on the mainland when I was a kid," I said. "But it hurt too much and I told my parents I wouldn't go anymore a couple years ago. I don't leave the island very often anymore."

Mara lowered her camera, her eyebrows raised. "But you could go to the other islands, couldn't you? You would be able to survive traveling along the coastline."

"I don't really see the point. I'm still stuck."

Mara opened her mouth, but voices caught our attention. A group of people broke through the heavy fog along the shoreline. As they drew closer, my stomach clenched and my body tensed.

Elizabeth walked with Jackie and Kyle, and another guy, Mark from school. Kyle had his arm slung around Elizabeth's shoulder, keeping her body tucked close to his. Apparently, that little thing between them was back on again.

My teeth ached with how hard I grit them together.

They caught sight of us when they were only a few feet away and their expressions changed to hostility. Elizabeth looked at Mara, her eyes never glancing my way, as if she could pretend I didn't exist and the time we'd spent together had never happened.

"What are you doing here, shark bait?" Jackie sneered.

Mara ignored them and studied her camera. "Let's go somewhere else," she said to me. "Somewhere a little more private."

Elizabeth's eyebrows drew together in a tight scowl at Mara's words. "There's no such thing as privacy around here," she said. "This is Swans Landing. Everyone knows what you do."

Not everything, I thought, suppressing a smug grin.

"We're not doing anything that concerns you," I said. "Go somewhere else to do whatever it is you're doing."

"This is our island, Fish Boy," Kyle said, stepping toward me. "Why don't you go off and swim with the crabs?"

Jackie and Mark laughed, but Elizabeth glared at me with apprehension etched into her features. What, did she think I'd spill her little secret to these guys? Like I wanted Mara to hear about it. Maybe if she hadn't been there, I'd take pleasure in seeing the fury on Kyle's face when he heard it had been me with my hands on Elizabeth the day before. But for now, I'd keep my mouth shut and my secrets to myself.

"Clever," I told him. "Did you think that up all by yourself?"

Elizabeth grabbed Kyle's arm. "Come on," she said. "Let's go somewhere else. They're not worth it anyway." She cast a sneer over her shoulder at Mara.

"Oh, no, *please* don't go," Mara said, rolling her eyes. "What will we do without your company to remind us what scum we are?"

Elizabeth's gaze finally met mine. She kept my gaze for a long moment, then finally turned, pulling Kyle by the hand behind her. "Come on," she ordered. "Let's get away from the stench. I can't stand fish."

Mara scowled as they walked away. "I'm aching to punch her in the mouth again," she muttered.

I kicked at the sand under my feet. "Maybe she's misunderstood."

Mara stared at me like I'd grown another head. "Oh, please. It doesn't take much to figure her out. Spoiled, self-centered brat."

I resisted the urge to look back to where Elizabeth and her friends had disappeared. We were from two different worlds, and we had no allegiance to each other. I didn't care who she messed around with.

"Maybe she's like us, but is too afraid to step outside the boundaries around here," I said.

Mara wrinkled her nose. "Are you actually defending her? Elizabeth Connors, the girl who has made your best friend miserable?"

My gaze darted toward the beach, where I could still see four dark specks growing smaller in the distance. Then I shook my head. "No, of course not. Elizabeth's not my problem."

Chapter 7

My body ached with the need to stay close to the water. Reed had already left for school ahead of me, eager to find his place among the soccer team before the first bell. I was lagging so far behind that even Mara had gone on without me. I was a good student, not a genius or anything, but I made good grades in all my classes. The problem was that sitting in those classrooms all day felt so stifling. Some days, especially near the new moon when the pull of the water was the strongest, I felt like I'd suffocate if I had to sit inside the concrete walls.

My feet had turned off the path before I realized where I was going. If I was lucky, Reed wouldn't find out I wasn't in school. He'd tell our parents for sure, unless I could bribe him before he had a chance. I needed a day to clear my head. One last day on my own before tourist season started and I had to be even more careful.

The silence and stillness that hung over the island among the gray clouds made it almost impossible to imagine tourists coming this year. Already I'd heard people talk about how their businesses might not survive if the tourists didn't come soon. Something felt different, something other than the weather, but I couldn't figure out what it was.

I emerged from the narrow path on the other side of the maritime forest to the little strip of beach where the ocean and sound met at the tip of the island. The water churned and the wind blasted across the sand. I sat down just out of reach of the foamy water that rushed onshore. Seagulls squawked overhead, swooping low to see if I had any food and then soaring away when they realized I wasn't going to feed them. I closed my eyes and breathed the salt that hung thick in the air.

A chill crept over me, but I pulled my shirt off to absorb what little sun broke through the clouds. I scanned the horizon as far as I could see into the fog as I sat in the sand, digging my fingers into the golden grains. There was nothing on the water. Ships only passed by far out to sea, rarely ever stopping at this island. The only people who really used this beach were the finfolk, once a month during song night.

I stared at the rippling water as hard as I could, looking for signs of life. But there was nothing other than the birds swooping over the water in search of fish.

"Where are you, Sailor?" I asked aloud. "Are you even still alive?"

Only the sound of the waves crashing toward shore and the calls of the birds answered me.

After a while, I got up and slipped out of my jeans. I tossed my boxers onto the sand and then made my way into the water. It was still cold enough to shock me a little as the water hit my legs, but I pushed myself farther.

Only a short distance in, the change overtook me and I let myself slip fully underwater. The cracking and popping of my bones felt in a way like some kind of bittersweet release. I didn't know how something could be so painful and pleasant at the same time. Despite the few minutes of agony, my body still craved this change.

I swam for a while, diving as far down into the water as I could and fighting against the rough current that tried to push me back toward shore. I dared a few flips, breaking the surface and arcing through the air before diving back down.

When I turned back toward the shore, shaking water from my eyes, I caught sight of a figure standing on the beach. Brown hair whipped around her head in a dark halo. She held one hand to her forehead to shield her eyes as she looked toward me.

For a moment, I let myself think it was someone else waiting there on shore, as she had many times before. I let myself believe briefly that this summer wouldn't be so bleak.

But then I pushed that thought away and headed toward shore. I stopped only a few yards out, studying Elizabeth as she stood knee deep in the water. We looked at each other for a long moment in silence.

Finally, she smirked. "Nice boxers," she said, nodding her head toward my clothes.

I admired the lean, muscled look of her legs

protruding from her cut-off jeans. "Nice legs." I'd never been good at flirting, but there was something different about Finfolk Dylan that made me do things Human Dylan never would.

"I suppose you don't have any of those right now, huh?" Elizabeth asked.

I laid back in the water, letting my tail fin flip and splash water toward her. The scales shone a brilliant blue in the sunlight before disappearing back under the water.

Elizabeth didn't even protest when the water sprayed across her, leaving a big wet spot on her shirt. Her eyes were wide as she stared at the water. "How do you do that?"

"What?"

She gestured toward me. "Grow a tail and scales."

I shrugged. "It's just what happens."

I started toward shore, ready to shed my finfolk form and be human again, but Elizabeth held up her hands.

"Wait." She waded deeper into the water, fighting to stand up in the rushing waves. "I've...I've never seen a finfolk up close like this before."

It seemed strange that she had lived her whole life on the island without seeing a finfolk up close, though it wasn't entirely unbelievable. Her father didn't like finfolk, so when would Elizabeth have ever had the chance to be around one in the water?

I extended a hand toward her. "Come on."

She hesitated, looking down at the water around her legs. It was up to her thighs now and she wobbled as she tried to keep her balance.

"I'll hold onto you," I promised. "I'll keep you above water."

She bit her lip, then walked toward me, reaching her hand until our fingertips touched. I entwined my fingers in hers, pulling her toward me. When she couldn't touch the bottom anymore, I wrapped my other arm around her waist to pull her close and keep her head above the surface.

We were so close, I could see the tiny golden flecks in her eyes. Her hair spread out on top of the water like octopus tentacles. Her teeth chattered slightly, but she didn't make any movement back toward shore.

"Can I touch your tail?" Elizabeth asked quietly.

I swallowed. "Go ahead."

Her hand slid down my chest, her fingers fluttering over my stomach. I suppressed a shudder when her palm pressed against the area where skin became scales as a warm tingle spread through me.

"I've never touched a...someone like you," she said. "It's different than I expected."

"What did you think it would feel like?" I asked.

Elizabeth tilted her head to one side. "Like a fish. But you're more...I don't know. Smooth."

I couldn't help laughing. This whole situation, being here in the water with Elizabeth, was so strange and unexpected. It felt like at any moment I'd blink and find it was all a hallucination. She would still be Elizabeth Connors, the girl who lived to torment finfolk, and I would be invisible Dylan Waverly again.

"Why are you here?" I asked.

"Do you want me to leave?" She moved closer, running her hand over my skin and scales again. "Do you want me to stop?"

I fought against the wave of tingles that shot through

me at her touch. "I'm serious. Why are you out here with me? You've always been the biggest bitch in school toward Sailor and Mara and me. And now, you're hiding out with me, sneaking around behind everyone's back?"

Elizabeth pulled back from me. She slipped under the surface for a moment, then came back up, sputtering. She glared at me through the rivers of water trickling from her hair. "If you don't want me here, I'll go."

She started back toward the shore, but with my tail, I was much faster than she could ever hope to be. I darted through the water, surfacing in front of her. The wide-eyed expression on her face showed I'd surprised her. In that moment, Elizabeth Connors looked something I had never seen in her before: vulnerable.

So I let myself be a little vulnerable too and told her the truth.

"I don't want to you go."

Water dripped down her face and off her chin, disappearing into the foaming waves around her shoulders. I reached for her hand and she didn't pull away.

"Do you trust me?" I asked.

She bit her lip, then nodded. "Yes."

"Hold your breath." I entwined my fingers in hers as she sucked in a huge gulp of air. Then I arced toward the water, pulling her with me and letting our two worlds merge into one.

Chapter 8

"The catches are getting better," Lake said brightly as he hauled another crab pot to the boat and tossed it over the side. It landed at my feet, spraying my ankles with salt water. The crabs inside scuttled over each other, their claws tangled as they snapped furiously at being wrenched from the bottom of the sound.

Lake treaded water next to the boat, bobbing along on the mostly still surface. It was seven A.M. and I had to be at school in an hour and a half. I didn't always come out with Lake to bring in catches before school since it was an exhausting job, but I liked doing it when I could. I'd stay as long as possible, then Lake would drop me back off on shore and I'd race to Swans Landing School, smelling like crabs and salt.

I dumped the crabs from the wire pot into the giant plastic bin in Lake's boat, then rebaited the pot and tossed it back into the water. "We're almost full," I said, surveying the plastic bin where the crabs fought and walked all over each other. The catch was picking up as the water warmed, but it had been a while since we'd had a catch this good.

Lake pulled himself from the water, expertly hopping over the side of the boat even with his finfolk tail. The golden scales faded and drew back into his skin as he shook the water off himself.

"Maybe this is a good sign," Lake said, pulling on his shorts once he had legs again. "If the sea life is returning to the area, the industry will pick up again."

I knew Lake hoped desperately things would pick up, like most everyone else in Swans Landing did. The tourists weren't the only beings that had become rare around our island. Without the fish or the tourists, it was a struggle to hang on around here.

At least with the humans, they had more options. We finfolk were stuck looking for other coastal towns where we could blend in. Or else, the finfolk homeland, which no one we knew had ever found.

With our bin nearly overflowing with crabs, Lake turned the boat around and headed back toward the sound side dock. The clouds had thinned today and the sun turned the sky pinkish orange as it rose over the island ahead of us. Most people hadn't started their day yet and I closed my eyes, reveling in the peacefulness of the morning. The air was silent except for the steady rumble of Lake's boat. For a moment, I could forget all of my problems with girls and my worries about Miss Gale and whether I smelled as bad as I thought I did.

But a moment never lasted long. As we pulled into

the dock, we were greeted by the sight of a familiar larger fishing boat already docked there. I could make out the white lettering on the back as we drew closer: *The Lizzie.* Elizabeth Connors's dad's boat.

Mr. Connors stood on the bow of his boat, an old baseball cap pulled low on his forehead atop a deep scowl that he kept aimed our way as Lake maneuvered his smaller, older boat next to the dock.

I hopped out, trying to ignore the feel of Mr. Connors's glare on my back as I tied the rope in place.

"That boat of yours looks even more pathetic every time I see it, Westray," Mr. Connors called, his voice deep and growling. "Why don't you put it out of its misery and sink it in the sound? It'd make a better artificial reef than fishing boat."

The men who worked for Mr. Connors laughed at this. Lake didn't respond as he hefted the plastic bin over the side of the boat toward me. It was heavy, but I managed not to drop it as I set it down on the dock.

Mr. Connors's ears turned red as he took in the sight of all those crabs in our catch. He gritted his teeth, his fists clenched. Like everyone else in Swans Landing, Mr. Connors's business had been hit by the decline of the sea life in the area.

"You'd better hope none of those came from my pots, Westray," Mr. Connors growled.

"I don't steal, Connors," Lake told him, brushing his still wet hair out of his face.

Mr. Connors made a grunting noise. "Your kind has always gotten their way by stealing from the good people of the lands they take over. I'm watching you, and the moment I have proof you're stealing from my pots, I will have the sheriff knocking on your door faster than green grass through a goose."

Lake picked up one end of the bin and I picked up the other. Between us, we carried the heavy load up the dock to the parking lot where Lake's Jeep waited. I was eager to get away from Mr. Connors. He'd always made me nervous, but now my skin felt itchy, like maybe he would be able to see the trace of Elizabeth's touch on me. I breathed a sigh of relief when I heard Mr. Connors rev his engine behind us and then pull away from the marina.

"I hope he catches something today," I said as we loaded the bin into the back of the Jeep. While I was at school, Lake would go around to restaurants on the island to try to sell as much of the catch as he could, then the ones left he'd send to a buyer he had on the mainland. "Or else he'll really think you stole from his pots."

"Harry Connors is always looking for something to blame me for. He always has, for as long as I've known him."

"Why?" I asked. "What does he have against you?"

Lake exhaled, blowing hair out of his face. "He thinks I stole something from him, long ago. I didn't, but it's easier for him to blame me than to admit his own faults."

"What does he think you stole?" I asked.

Lake closed the back door of his Jeep. "Shouldn't you be getting to school?"

The sun was getting high in the sky. I dreaded another day stuck inside Swans Landing School instead of out on the water.

I sighed. "I guess so. I'll see you this afternoon."

* * *

"Mr. Waverly!"

I stopped in the hall and turned to find Mr. Richter, the school guidance counselor, making his way toward me among the students streaming out the front doors. The last bell had rung and I was full of jittery nerves. All I could think about was going to Pirate's Cove to see if Elizabeth would be there again.

"Yes, sir?" I asked when he approached. Mr. Richter was pretty young compared to most of the teachers and staff at Swans Landing School, but old enough that he was not exactly as "cool" as he thought he was.

"I was hoping I could speak with you for a few minutes," Mr. Richter said, giving me a pat on the shoulder. "Would you mind joining me in my office?"

I wanted to run, to break free of this gray building and breathe the salt air. I had been cooped up inside for too long, and the end of the day was always draining until I could smell the ocean again.

But I nodded and followed Mr. Richter back to his office.

I sat down in the squeaky blue chair as Mr. Richter settled himself down behind his desk. He leaned back in his seat, his hands folded behind his head. "So, Dylan," he began, "I wanted to talk to you about your college decisions."

I raised my eyebrows. "What about them?"

"Well," Mr. Richter said slowly, "have you made any yet?"

Mr. Richter had spoken with all of the juniors this year, giving us various brochures from colleges across the country. Mine had been tossed in the trash three months ago.

"No," I answered.

Mr. Richter sat up, placing his hands on his desk. "Dylan, this is your future we're talking about. You're a good student. You'd do well in furthering your education—"

"Mr. Richter?" I shifted in my seat, glancing up at one of those inspiring posters of the night sky with the words REACH FOR THE STARS under it. "You...you know *what* I am?"

Mr. Richter was quiet for a moment before answering. "Yes, I know."

"So why are we having this conversation?" I asked.

Mr. Richter leaned over his desk. "Dylan, you can't sell yourself short because you think you're tied to this island. Finfolk or not, you still have the chance to do whatever you want in your life."

I laughed. "I'm sorry, Mr. Richter, but you have no idea what it's like to be me. I can't survive away from the ocean. I physically ache and get sick. I'm stuck here."

"There are schools near the coast. You could—"

I shook my head as I stood. "Thanks, Mr. Richter. But my future is here, making a life on the water. It's what people like me do."

"And what will you do when that life dries up?" Mr. Richter asked.

I paused at the door, my hand on the knob.

"The fish are disappearing, Dylan," Mr. Richter said. "You know that much better than I do."

"Lake and I pulled in a good catch this morning," I said. "Maybe that means things are getting better."

"It's May and the tourists haven't started coming."

I shrugged. "It's a cycle, right?"

But Mr. Richter looked grim when I glanced back at him. He stood from his desk and walked toward me.

"Did you know the ferry missed its scheduled stop this morning?" He slipped his hands into his pockets and rocked back on his heels. "It just didn't come. When someone at the dock here called the mainland dock, the person spoke as if they'd never heard of Swans Landing before. Like they didn't remember the island." He paused. "Like it didn't exist."

A chill prickled its way up my spine. "That's ridiculous."

Mr. Richter stared back at me. "Is it? A lot of things on this island are ridiculous, and yet..." He reached past me and pulled the door open. "Maybe it was a mistake. Maybe you're right and things are getting better. But don't throw your future away because you think you're stuck here, Dylan. There's a whole world out there, and a lot more water than what touches these shores. I don't know what's happening here, but don't let yourself be forgotten along with the island."

Mr. Richter's words left me feeling slightly rattled. When I stepped outside into the thick gray afternoon, I felt chilled all the way through.

I had lived my entire life on the island. The sound of the ferry's horn as it approached and disembarked from the island was a constant part of the background noise. The ferry traveled the three hour path between Swans Landing and the mainland three times a day.

Why had I not noticed that the horn didn't break the silence while we were on the water? My thoughts had been absorbed in Elizabeth Connors, that was why. She had been the last thing I'd thought about as I'd fallen asleep the night before and the first thing in my mind that morning when I opened my eyes.

Instead of turning toward the road that would take me to Pirate's Cove, I followed the sandy street to my own neighborhood. Two old women drove by in a golf cart, giving me suspicious stares as they passed. A group of kids played soccer in the middle of the road. A woman bounced a baby in her lap as they rocked on a wooden swing on the front porch of a house at the corner. Everything looked the same as it always had.

Except there were no tourists.

And apparently, no ferry either.

Chapter 9

"Let's take a break." I sat up, pushing tangled hair out of my eyes.

The thin strap of Elizabeth's tank top slipped down one shoulder. "Getting too warm for you?" she asked, smirking my way.

I licked my dry lips, still tasting her strawberry lip gloss. I didn't know what was going on in my head anymore. Here I was, sitting on Elizabeth's bed, in her room. Her parents weren't home. She didn't say much when I asked where they were, she had shrugged and said, "Working." She had a younger brother and sister, but she didn't say where they were either.

It was just the two of us, alone here in her quiet house. I didn't want to think about her family or mine, or about the rest of Swans Landing at all. The ferry had come that morning as scheduled, but even that hadn't settled the strange feeling in my gut. Like there was something happening here that none of us could see. Not just the missing ferry or the clouds that wouldn't lift or the tourists that didn't come.

But I didn't want to think about any of that right then. Any other guy in my position would lie back and enjoy it.

The room smelled like her and looked like her. Coral colored bedding and sheer lacy curtains. Pictures of her friends were taped on the wall next to me, a giant collage of all the people at school I spent my days avoiding.

"I feel a little creeped out with all of your boyfriends watching us." I nodded toward the pictures on the wall.

"Number one, they're not my boyfriends. Number two." Elizabeth moved in front of me, sliding herself between my legs. "You're the only one here with me."

She tried to press her lips to mine again, but I turned my head so her mouth met my cheek. "And how many of them have been here before me?"

Elizabeth drew back, rising up on her knees. She crossed her arms and glared at me. "What do you think I am, Dylan?"

I shrugged. "I don't know. Isn't that the whole point? I barely know you at all, right?"

She wrinkled her nose. "So what? You want to talk? Fine. Talk."

I pushed myself off the bed and grabbed my shoes, shoving my feet into them. "Maybe I should go."

But Elizabeth wrapped her arms around me, one hand slipping down my collar to my chest. Her mouth was near my ear, her breath hot on my skin. "Don't go," she whispered.

I didn't move. We sat there for a moment, her body pressed against my back. I had asked myself a hundred times on the way to her house what I was doing, and I still didn't have an answer. All I knew was I couldn't stay away.

"None of them have been here before," she told me.

I snorted.

"I'm serious. You're the first guy who's been in my room."

"What about Kyle?"

She laughed. "He wishes."

I wanted to believe she was telling the truth. "What makes me so special?" I asked.

She slipped her body around me until she was in my lap, her arms around my neck. "Because you're different."

"Because I'm finfolk? You have some kind of fetish?"

Elizabeth scowled. "No. *You*. You're different than all those other guys at school. Not just the finfolk thing. Everything." She broke off and looked away, biting her lip as if she had said too much. For a moment, she had opened herself up in a way I had never seen. I wanted to see more of that, but already her expression seemed to be shutting down and returning to her usual detached state.

"So, Fish Boy," she said, "what do you want to know about me?"

I wanted to know everything about her, but I could tell she wasn't willing to get too personal. "What's your favorite color?" I asked.

Elizabeth rolled her eyes, but she said, "Coral. Yours?"

"Blue. Favorite food?"

"The lasagna from the Sand Dollar."

I nodded. "That is good. Mine would have to be Miss Gale's chicken pastry."

Elizabeth trailed a finger over my jaw. "Are we done yet?" she asked.

My gaze scanned the room, trying to find something to distract me from the sensations her touch sent through my body. A miniature version of the Eiffel Tower stood on top of a book of Shakespeare on her desk. "You like Shakespeare?"

She sighed. "Yes, I like Shakespeare."

"Let me guess," I said. "*Romeo and Juliet.*"

She tilted her head back, tossing her hair behind her shoulder as she said, "No. *The Tempest.*"

"Which one is that?" I asked.

"The one about the people on the island."

I frowned. "Oh." I'd had enough of islands to last me ten thousand lifetimes. Change of subject. "Have you ever been to Paris?"

She followed my gaze, then shook her head. "No, that's from Las Vegas."

"When did you go to Vegas?"

"Three years ago," she said, shrugging. "Family vacation. My mom always wanted to go."

The farthest my family had ever been was Manteo, farther north along the Outer Banks. It was difficult to do family vacations for us. We couldn't go inland, and if we stayed near the coast, we got the urge to swim, which was dangerous in places where no one knew about finfolk.

"Where else have you been?" I asked.

She named several trips, some near the coast and others far inland. I tried to imagine all the places she had seen, the ones I'd only experienced through pictures and movies.

"My turn," she said. Elizabeth's body stiffened slightly and she stared hard at me. "Why didn't you go with Sailor when she left? I thought you two were stuck at the hip."

My finger traced circles over her thigh while I thought about this.

"Sometimes I think I should have gone," I admitted. "I had a way out of here, away from this island, and I gave it up. But I don't want to find more finfolk. I don't want to swim forever. I've spent my life swimming and sometimes I'm so sick of it. Sometimes I want to walk for the rest of my life."

"I thought all of you people liked being finfolk."

"Sailor once called it a half-life," I told her. "And she's right. We live with a constant ache for what we don't have. If we're in the water, we want to be on land. If we're on land, we want the water. It never ends."

"I think it would be fun." Elizabeth shifted in my lap, moving closer to me. "To change, and be something else for a while. Leave everything behind and swim far away."

I didn't want to be Finfolk Dylan right then. I wanted the chance to imagine being a normal guy. So I turned myself around, pushing Elizabeth down onto the bed and moving over her. I kissed her hungrily, feeling like I could never get enough.

She grinned up at me when I pulled back so we could catch our breaths. "So, what about you? How many girlfriends have you ended up with like this?"

Mara's sleeping in my bed didn't count. We had kissed only a little, and I'd been too afraid to touch her, thinking if I did it would break whatever moment we'd had. That she'd realize I wasn't the one she wanted after all. Which had happened anyway, despite me keeping my hands to myself.

"None," I told her. "Not like this."

Chapter 10

Mara smiled wide when she opened her front door. My stomach still did a little flip-flop whenever she smiled at me. I hadn't talked much to her these last few days. Sneaking off with Elizabeth during lunch and after school had taken up a lot of my time. It was nice to see Mara again.

"Dylan!" Lake called from his table in front of the windows. "Come see the masterpieces."

He had a table full of shadow boxes laid out side by side and each one contained an angel made of seashells. They were all created from the same types of shells, but each was a unique blend of colors. Usually I envied Lake for how easily he could create amazing works of art from ordinary things, but today I felt nothing.

"They're great," I said, trying to gather up some enthusiasm.

"I thought I'd make a bunch of them for summer this year," Lake said. "They will be the center of my display. You know how tourists love things like this."

"Yes, cheap and tacky, they'll love them," Mara said.

Lake shot her an annoyed glare. "You want food this summer, you better hope my cheap and tacky angels sell."

"Like you even know how to cook food in the first place," Mara shot back with a mischievous smile.

Any other time, I would have laughed and enjoyed seeing the two of them teasing each other. Mara and Lake's relationship had been so strained since she arrived in Swans Landing, so it was nice that they were bonding. But I couldn't get into the same light-hearted mood they had.

"Did you hear the ferry didn't come yesterday?" I asked, my gaze focused on one of the angels.

Lake and Mara paused, looking at me.

"What?" Lake asked.

"Mr. Richter told me the ferry didn't come to the island yesterday morning," I said. "And when the guy at the dock called to find out why, the person there acted as though they'd never heard of Swans Landing before."

I looked up to see how they'd take this news. Mara looked confused, tilting her head to the side as she absorbed my words. Lake pressed his lips together.

"What does that mean?" Mara asked.

I shrugged. "I don't know. That's what Mr. Richter told me."

We looked at Lake, but he only shook his head. "Maybe it was someone new," he said. "Maybe he was confused."

"Has the ferry ever not come?" Mara asked.

A few seconds of silence ticked by before Lake answered, "No, except during hurricanes."

The day outside the window was dark and cloudy, but it didn't feel like a hurricane. It didn't feel like anything I'd ever experienced before.

Mara shook her head. "I'm sure it was all a mistake. Mr. Richter must have heard wrong." She walked across the room and picked up her camera. "I'm going over to see Miss Gale. Dylan, you want to come?"

I followed Mara down the steps and then we walked side by side toward Miss Gale's house only a couple streets over. I hoped Mara couldn't smell the scent of Elizabeth's perfume that still lingered on my clothes.

In the distance, beyond the homes of our neighborhood, I could hear the ever present swish of the ocean as it lapped at the shore. Sometimes I could tune it out, but I always felt its presence deep inside me. Mr. Richter and the other humans on the island had no idea what it was like to be finfolk and to be connected to the island in the way we were. Leaving would be easy for them.

"So what do you think?" I asked, breaking the silence between us.

"About what?" Mara pulled her hair back from her face and tied it up in a messy bun.

"About the ferry not coming."

"It's probably like Lake said. Just a misunderstanding."

I kicked at a rock. "Mr. Richter said we're being forgotten."

"What does he mean by that?"

"The tourists haven't come. Now the ferry didn't come." I kicked at a flattened soda can in the road. "What if Mr. Richter is right?"

Mara gave me a look like I was being stupid. "Like what, the whole island is disappearing off the earth? Don't be ridiculous, Dylan."

Ridiculous. *A lot of things on this island are ridiculous,* Mr. Richter had said. I grew scales and a fin whenever I was in salt water. Why couldn't an entire island disappear if it wanted to?

We knocked on Miss Gale's door, but we didn't expect an answer. I unlocked it and we stepped inside the cool house. The only light came from the skylights overhead, but it was so muted and gray that the crystal prisms didn't cast any rainbows that day.

"Miss Gale?" Mara called as I followed her down the hall to Miss Gale's room.

Miss Gale was sitting up in bed, the blanket pushed back off her legs. Her shoulders were stooped and her chest heaved as she panted, as if she had run a marathon.

"Oh," she said, seeing us in the doorway. "I was going to get something to drink."

"Lay down," Mara told her, rushing across the room to help Miss Gale settle into bed again. "We'll get you a drink. Dylan?"

I nodded and left the room to get a glass of water from the kitchen. When I returned, Mara was tucking Miss Gale into bed.

"I should go to the store," Miss Gale said. "Jim needs me."

"Mr. Moody is fine," I assured her. "I'm helping out this summer."

"Oh, Lord have mercy," Miss Gale moaned, closing her eyes. "Please tell me you're not messing up my food counter. It took me ages to get everything where I wanted it."

I smiled. "No, ma'am, I haven't touched it. Mr. Moody has been doing the cooking."

Miss Gale moaned again. "That's what I was afraid of most!"

"Then you'll have to get better," Mara said. "So you can go back and chase him away from your counter."

Mara grinned at me and I tried not to laugh. It wasn't a laughing situation at all, with Miss Gale as sick as she was, but Mara's smile could make me forget everything else.

Another smile flashed through my head for a moment and tingles spread over my body.

"Dylan?"

I blinked, focusing my thoughts on Mara in front of me. She looked at me like she was waiting for an answer to a question I hadn't heard.

"What?"

Mara heaved a sigh and then shook her head. "Never mind. I'll get it."

She left the room, leaving me standing by the bed, still holding the glass of salt water. Miss Gale's head had fallen to the side and her eyes were closed. She breathed softly in her sleep. I set the glass down on the table next to her bed, then stepped out of the room.

I had intended to find Mara and see if she needed help with whatever she was doing, but instead, my gaze fell on the door across from Miss Gale's. It was closed and had probably been closed for the last two months.

The door squeaked a little when I opened it. I stepped into the darkened room, breathing in the familiar scent. *Sailor.* If I closed my eyes, I could feel her all around me. The room was full of her and of the memories I had with her. Her fiddle sat on a chair in the corner, now coated with a layer of dust. Her clothes were still tossed around the floor, as if she had changed out of them that day.

On the dresser was a framed picture of the two of us. We were ten in the picture, and both of us held up crabs, dangling by one claw, as we grinned wide for the camera.

I set the picture back down in its place and then crossed the room to Sailor's bed. She still had the same yellow comforter she'd had for years, with the same goldfish shaped pillow tossed on top of it. I laid back on the bed, breathing deeply as I turned my face toward the pillows.

"What are you doing in here?"

I sat up, startled. Mara stood in the doorway, a blanket clutched in her arms.

"I was just..." I let my voice trail off, shrugging. "What are you doing?"

"Miss Gale seems cold, so I went to find another blanket." She stepped into the room, looking around cautiously, as if she expected Sailor to jump out at her at any moment.

The goldfish pillow tumbled off the bed as I leaped to my feet. "Oh, okay. We should give it to her then."

But Mara didn't move. Her gaze scanned over the room before settling on me again.

"You feel closer to her here, don't you?" she asked, her voice sad and small.

I dug my hands into my pockets and nodded. "I spent a lot of time with her here."

My cheeks flamed at the smirk Mara gave me.

"Not like that," I said quickly. "I mean, we hung out here a lot. I used to spend the night with Sailor all the time when we were kids. We'd always get into trouble with Miss Gale." I laughed as a memory sprang into my mind. "Once, we got into Miss Gale's cold cream that she always used at night. She said it was for keeping wrinkles away, so we tried to put it on a lizard Sailor had found outside. When Miss Gale found out, she chased us both up and down the street, threatening to whip our behinds if she caught us."

Mara smiled, though I could see the sadness in her eyes. "I wish I had memories like that with Josh. Sometimes I feel like I don't have anything, like maybe it was all a dream. Maybe he'll come back and things won't be the same as they were." She swallowed, blinking quickly.

I hugged her, pulling her close. She tensed at first, but then she relaxed and laid her head on my chest.

It was what I had wanted for months now, to be this close to her. But it felt wrong somehow.

After a moment, she pulled away. "I think I'm going to stay here with Miss Gale tonight," she said.

"I'll stay too," I said quickly. "To keep you company."

Mara rolled her eyes. "Sure, because the couch looks big enough for both of us."

I gestured toward the bed. "I'm sure Sailor won't mind if we use her bed. It won't be the first time we've slept together."

I meant it as a joke, but the look in Mara's eyes told

me I'd stepped over a line she had refused to cross. We hadn't spoken about that one night she had spent in my bed.

But we were supposed to be friends. I was a nice guy. I could keep my hands to myself. Well, maybe not with Elizabeth, but this was Mara. I'd been a perfect little gentleman before. I could probably do it again for one night.

"Dylan," Mara started.

But I didn't want to hear the "Let's be friends" speech for the hundredth time.

"Sharing a bed with me doesn't mean you're cheating on Josh," I said.

"I know that," Mara snapped. "But it's complicated."

"It's just sleeping! The couch is lumpy, the bed would be much more comfortable. And so what if something did happen? Would that be so terrible? Am I repulsive?"

Mara shook her head and started to turn, but I grabbed her arm, pulling her back to face me.

"Josh *left* you, if you hadn't noticed," I said through clenched teeth. "*I'm* the one who's still here. I'm the one who has listened to you and held you when you cried these last couple of months. Don't I get anything for that? No, because you think you're in love with a guy who didn't even care enough to stick around. A guy who might not even still be alive."

Mara's eyes widened and her mouth dropped open. She stared at me, frozen for a moment. Then anger clouded her face and she pulled her arm from my grasp.

"I think you should leave," she said, her mouth tight.

I reached toward her, feeling terrible for what I'd said. I didn't want Josh dead. I might not exactly like the guy, but I'd never want him dead. He had to keep Sailor safe until she came home.

"Mara, I—"

But she stepped away from me, turning her head. "Just go," she said, her chin quivering slightly.

I stood there for a moment longer, but she refused to look at me.

"Fine," I growled. Ducking my head, I walked past her and headed down the hall.

Chapter 11

The agitation I'd felt about the things going on around the island added fuel to the frustration now coursing through my body after my fight with Mara.

I didn't want to be one of those guys who got angry over little things, but I was tired of being the nice, invisible guy I'd always been. I had tried being nice to everyone. I had tried not drawing attention to myself. I had tried to go along with what everyone else wanted, and what did it get me? Mara chose Josh over me, even when he wasn't here. Elizabeth was happy to keep our relationship a secret while she paraded around with those imbeciles she called friends.

I was still invisible Dylan Waverly. I was still stuck.

I walked with my head down, kicking at small rocks and broken seashells that littered the path along Swans Landing's main road. An engine revved behind me, drawing closer, but I didn't look up until the ATV skidded to a stop in front of me.

"What's a little fish doing so far from the water?" Kyle McCutcheon snarled.

I glared at Kyle, then turned and started walking in the opposite direction.

The ATV's engine roared as Kyle revved it, then he sped around me, swerving so he blocked my path. A cloud of sand billowed around us as he leaned over the handlebars, sneering at me.

"I'm talking to you, Fish Boy," Kyle growled. "You think that stunt you pulled at the dock was funny?"

"It was one of my better moves," I told him.

Kyle revved the engine. "You'd better watch it, Waverly, or I'm going to kick your ass one of these days."

I held out my arms wide. "Why wait? I'm right here, McCutcheon."

Kyle's jaw twitched as he studied me. He revved the engine again, as if he thought it was menacing. "You're lucky I have something to do today."

But I wasn't in the mood to back down. Adrenaline pumped through me, turning my frustration into a burning rage. I wanted to hit something, to feel the release of action, and Kyle's face looked like as good a punching bag as any.

I leaned over the ATV, pushing at his shoulders. "Come on. Do it."

"Don't touch me, freak." Kyle spat at the ground near my feet.

I lunged at him, wrapping one arm around his neck and ripping him off the ATV. Caught by surprise, he slammed into the sandy asphalt, his head smacking the ground with a crack. I was on top of him immediately, swinging my fists to connect with any part of his body I could reach. It felt good, this release of energy. The sound of my knuckles smashing against Kyle's face urged me on.

It didn't take Kyle long to fight back. He kicked at me, pushing me off him enough that he could get up and gain the upper hand. He threw me onto the street, knocking the air out of me for a moment. Kyle hovered over me, his right foot connecting with my stomach. I curled up, rolling onto my side and groaning as Kyle kicked me again.

"You little bastard," Kyle roared. "What did you think you'd do, huh? You think you can really take me, freak?"

I uncurled myself long enough to wrap my arms around Kyle's leg when he swung it my way again. I twisted his foot, pulling hard and knocking him off balance. Kyle tumbled to the ground next to me and I straddled his stomach, my fists once again swinging wildly at his face. I heard a crack and then a gush of blood oozed from Kyle's nose.

The sound of the ocean roared loud in my ears as I watched the blood drip down Kyle's cheek. My fists were frozen in mid-air and I felt exhausted and disconnected from what was happening.

My hesitation gave Kyle the advantage once again. He pushed me off of him and then rolled to his knees, lunging at me. I lay on the road, not even bothering to shield my face as Kyle pummeled his fist into my mouth and nose.

* * *

"Where have you been?" Elizabeth crossed her arms when I emerged from the trees at Pirate's Cove. Her face was twisted into a scowl, but my gaze was on the bikini top and tiny shorts she wore, her long tanned legs planted in the golden sand.

Elizabeth's eyes widened when she got a good look at me. She raced across the sand, her hand over her mouth.

"Oh my god, Dylan," she said. "You're bleeding. What happened?"

Sailor was gone. Mara treated me like she never trusted me. I didn't have anyone.

Except Elizabeth.

If Mara could spend her days crying over a guy who wasn't even here, I could spend mine forgetting about her with a girl who couldn't seem to stay away.

I closed the distance between us, my eyes locked on hers. I crushed my swollen mouth to hers, pressing my hand into the back of her head and wrapping my other arm around her waist to pull her as close as possible. She smelled like sand and tasted like coconut lip gloss. I pulled her up on her tiptoes, my tongue twisting around hers. My body ached from Kyle's beating, but the pain took away my ability to think about anything else.

Elizabeth looked dazed when she finally pulled back to catch her breath. "Whoa there, Fish Boy," she said, laughing shakily. "Where did that come from?"

I wasn't in the mood to talk. "Let's go swimming."

I kicked off my jeans and then pulled her into the water with me, sinking low into the rippling waves. The ache of the change started deep in my bones and I turned back to Elizabeth, kissing her again. I didn't want to let her go as my body shuddered and we slipped under the water, my bones popping and skin shredding into scales.

We resurfaced once the change was complete, Elizabeth coughing and gasping for air. "Some of us can't breathe underwater," she reminded me.

I pushed a lock of wet hair away from her face. "Be glad you can't."

Elizabeth laid back on the surface, stretching her arms out to the sides. "I thought you fish people all loved to be in the water." She squinted in the late afternoon sunlight. "Where were you anyway? And what happened to your face?"

I ignored her questions. "Sometimes I want things to be simple. To be one person instead of two."

"To be human?" Elizabeth asked.

I shrugged. "Maybe."

"Being human isn't always as simple as you think," Elizabeth said. "Sometimes even we have to be two people, whether we want to or not."

I studied her, thinking of the Elizabeth Connors I saw at school and the Elizabeth Connors that swam here with me now. How many different Elizabeths were there inside her?

And which one was real?

"What's this all about, Elizabeth?" I asked.

She blinked. "What?"

I gestured from her to me. "This. What is this about?"

She moved toward me, slipping her arms around my neck. "Whatever you want it to be about."

I pulled out of her grasp. "I'm not Kyle or one of

those other dumb guys that follows you around. Why are you doing this? What exactly are you getting out of playing around with me?"

She turned her head, looking at the surface of the water next to me. I wrapped my hands around her waist, helping to keep her head above the waves.

"I don't want to leave the island," she said at last.

"Why would you leave?"

She turned her gaze back to me, her forehead wrinkled into a deep scowl. "Because my daddy says we'll die if we stay here. The fish are disappearing, Dylan. The tourists aren't coming. The humans and the finfolk don't get along. People like your best buddy Lake Westray are driving my daddy out of business. We're going to have to leave to find work. We'll have to move."

My grip on her waist went slack for a moment and she slipped under. I quickly steadied her as she coughed out a mouthful of water.

"So you think if you mess around with me, I can convince Lake to do what? Let your daddy have all the good fishing spots?"

Elizabeth shot me a withering look. "Don't flatter yourself, Dylan. You're not that important in my daddy's eyes."

"Then what part do I play in this?" I asked.

Her eyes looked red, but I couldn't tell for sure if that was from tears or the salt water. "I'm sick of being afraid. I've grown up hearing my daddy tell me how bad all of you are. But Mara saved his life, and then that day at the dock, with Kyle, you stood up to him. For me." She swallowed, blinking quickly. "I thought maybe I could find a way to stay if we weren't all so afraid of each other."

I shook my head. "You have a chance I don't have. You can leave this island and find something better."

Elizabeth's jaw twitched. "I see all of you people swimming and fishing and living your lives as if the rest of us don't even exist. It doesn't matter if we're here or not, all of you will still manage to survive. You're tied to this island in a way we aren't. It's not fair. This is *my* home too."

I hated the way she said "you people," as if we were completely separate from her.

"So how do I fit into all of this?" I asked through clenched teeth.

Elizabeth's lips looked bluer than before. The water was too cold for her, and she'd need to go back to shore soon.

"I thought if I could get close to you, get to know you, then maybe you could help me fix the people on this island," she said. "Maybe we could convince Lake and my daddy to work together instead of fighting each other."

She spoke with that same Elizabeth Connors confidence I had always known. Beneath the girl who kissed me and looked at me as if she wanted nothing except me, she was still the same scheming, lying, manipulative person she'd always been.

And I was still just a pawn in her game. Something to help her get what she wanted.

"You need to get back to shore," I told her. I turned toward the beach, pulling her along beside me.

"Dylan," Elizabeth started, but a wave splashed water

into her mouth and she coughed.

I changed back to my human form as we drew close to shore, rising up on my legs to walk through the crashing surf. I let my arm drop from Elizabeth's waist. She struggled through the current next to me, but I didn't look her way.

"Dylan, listen to me—"

I grabbed my clothes from the beach and pulled them on, ignoring the sand that clung to them. "I'm done playing your game, Elizabeth. If that was all you ever wanted, all you had to do was talk to me. Not..." I gestured between us. "You didn't have to do all this."

"How else was I supposed to get close to you?"

"I'm a pretty reasonable guy, once you get to know me." I glanced at her. "If you ever bother getting to know me."

My feet slipped across the sand as I marched toward the tree line.

"Dylan, wait. It's not like that."

I didn't want to hear her lies. "You don't have to pretend anymore," I told her. "Go back to your friends and forget any of this happened."

She stopped, looking at me with glassy eyes. I resisted the urge to go to her and press my lips to hers one last time.

"What am I supposed to do now?" she asked. "My daddy is serious about leaving. This is my home."

"I don't care what you do. It's not my problem, is it?"

Elizabeth flinched, taking a step back.

"You don't even realize how lucky you are," I said, spitting the words with as much venom in my tone as I could. "You think I would choose a life stuck on a dying island? Do you think it's fun always choosing between the land and the water? Do you think I enjoy beatings from your boyfriends because of who I am?" I stalked away, putting distance between us. "Do us both a favor and get out of here. Don't be forgotten. Be human."

I left her as I slipped into the trees, my body aching from the effects of the water and her touch.

Chapter 12

My mom freaked out when she saw the aftermath of Kyle's fists on my face. She demanded to know who had done it, but I wouldn't tell. What was the point? She would either call his parents and cause even more problems, or she'd ignore it because of the strained human-finfolk relationship.

But this was Swans Landing, and nothing stayed secret for long. By the next morning, everyone knew. They stared as I walked across the lawn of the school. They whispered behind my back when I passed in the hall. I wasn't invisible anymore and I could feel all the stares burning holes into my skin. I sat in the back of all my classes, ignoring everyone else around me. At lunch, I went to the library so I wouldn't have to deal with them.

"Hey."

I looked up from the calculus homework I was working on to find Mara standing at the end of the table.

"Hey," I said.

"You look terrible," she told me.

I gave her a half-smile.

"Can I sit down?" she asked.

I shrugged. "If you want."

She slid into the seat across from me, dropping her backpack at her feet. "I'm really sorry about yesterday."

"It's fine," I told her, looking down at my paper. The numbers weren't making much sense and I hadn't been able to focus.

"No, it's not," Mara said. "I think we're both really stressed and worried, and we're taking it out on each other. Which isn't a good thing. I like you, Dylan, and I want to be friends."

Friends. I would always be the friend.

"I want to be friends too. I really didn't mean anything by suggesting we share the bed. It was supposed to be a joke."

Mara sighed. "I guess I'm not in a joking mood these days. Sorry."

"I'm sorry for what I said." I rolled my pencil back and forth on the table. "I don't want Josh dead, you know."

Mara nodded. "I know."

A laugh nearby caught my attention. Beyond Mara's shoulder, Elizabeth and Jackie walked through the library door. Elizabeth's gaze caught mine for a moment, but then she looked away quickly as she headed toward the computers.

Mara looked over her shoulder, then turned back to

me, rolling her eyes. "The Swans Landing Witch is in full-force today. In gym class, she kept calling me Tuna."

Elizabeth sat down at the end of the row of computers. She leaned over to say something to Jackie and then laughed again.

"Maybe she's under a lot of stress too," I said.

Mara wrinkled her nose. "What has gotten into you lately?"

"What do you mean?" I asked.

"That's the second time in two weeks you've defended Elizabeth Connors."

If I wasn't careful, Mara would figure out something had happened between Elizabeth and me. And on an island as small as Swans Landing, secrets were hard to keep. If one person could figure it out, eventually everyone would.

But did it matter anymore?

"Maybe I'm tired of fighting with humans," I said.

"We're not talking about humans," Mara told me. "We're talking about Elizabeth Connors. She's an entirely different species of her own."

As if on cue, Elizabeth and Jackie got up from the computers. They turned our way, Elizabeth leading the path toward our table, a smirk etched on her face.

"Hello, Tuna," she said to Mara. She barely glanced at me. "Fish Boy. I thought I smelled something rotten over here."

Mara sighed. "Your jokes are getting old, Elizabeth. Call me when you have some new material."

Elizabeth's smirk deepened as she glared down at Mara. "What's the matter? Upset your boyfriend ran off with a whale?"

"I guess you're still jealous that he chose me over you, huh?" Mara asked.

Jackie sucked in a gasp, her eyes wide as she looked at Mara. "Don't flatter yourself, Westray," she said. "Elizabeth could have had Josh if she really wanted him."

Elizabeth tossed her hair over her shoulder. "I have better things to do than play around with fish."

My hand clenched around my pencil, but I bit my lip to keep from speaking.

"Besides," Elizabeth snarled, "it doesn't matter anyway. He's probably dead now. I always knew you people were shark bait."

Mara leaped from her chair, her nose an inch from Elizabeth's. "One more word," she growled in a low voice. "And you'll get my foot up your—"

"Girls," Ms. Perez, the school librarian, hissed from her desk. "If you don't break it up right now, you'll all get a trip to the principal's office."

Elizabeth stepped back, giving Mara one last smirk. "See you later, Tuna."

She turned, ignoring me as if I didn't exist. I clenched my fist tighter, the pencil in my hand cracking. *Don't say anything.*

But I didn't listen to my own advice.

"Elizabeth," I said.

She stopped, her shoulders tensed. Jackie looked back at me, her eyebrows raised. Even Mara studied me with confusion etched on her face.

It was several long moments before Elizabeth turned around to face me. Her expression was neutral, but her eyes held a hint of fear.

"What do you want, Fish Boy?" Her voice dripped with contempt, as it always had whenever she spoke to me. She really was two entirely different people.

"Tell your idiot boyfriend I hope he enjoys the broken nose I gave him," I said.

Elizabeth wrinkled her nose, casting a disgusted look at me. "Tell him yourself." Then she spun on her heel and walked away, never once looking back at me.

Mara sat down again, tapping her fingers on the table. Seconds ticked by, but she didn't say anything. I couldn't meet her gaze. I kept my eyes focused on the jumble of numbers scratched across the page in front of me.

"Dylan?" Mara finally asked.

I forced myself to look up and meet her golden brown eyes. I could see the question there, on the tip of her tongue. I clenched my teeth, waiting for her to ask.

But instead, she said, "I think you killed your pencil."

I opened my hand, releasing the two pieces of broken pencil.

* * *

"Mutant freak."

"I can't believe he showed up today."

I buried my hands deep in my pockets, trying to block out the sounds of the voices around me, none of which were being quiet. They didn't care if I heard. They wanted me to hear. They wanted me to know I was not like them. I could walk the same halls they did and act as human as I wanted to, but I would never be the same as them.

I missed Sailor so much my chest felt hollow.

"Where do you think you're going, freak?"

Kyle and his friends stood in my way, fanned out in a line to block my path. They all had their arms crossed, matching scowls on their faces.

I tried to push between them, but Kyle and one of his friends pushed me backward. "I'm trying to get to class, dumbass," I told him.

Kyle stepped forward, sneering down at me. "My handiwork looks good on you, Fish Boy. Maybe I should do it again real soon."

I became aware of the audience around us. Movement in the hall had come to a complete stop and everyone watched the exchange between Kyle and me. I spotted Elizabeth standing with Jackie behind the line of guys. She stared at me, her green eyes wide and nervous.

I wanted to see the smile fall off Kyle's face when he heard what I'd been doing with Elizabeth these last few days. I wanted him to know that she had chosen me, the invisible Fish Boy, over him.

I could see it in her face, in the rigid way she stood. She was waiting for me to tell Kyle, to tell everyone what she had done. All I had to do was open my mouth, and I'd tear down the facade Elizabeth had carefully built around her. Maybe we really could change the way finfolk and humans in this school acted toward each other. We could break through the barriers.

Do you trust me? I had asked her.

Yes, she had said.

But she didn't really. Not fully. Maybe she had never really trusted anyone.

"What are you staring at?" Kyle asked. He pushed at my shoulder, breaking my lock on Elizabeth's gaze.

I focused on him, meeting his snarling glare with a calm, restrained smile. "I'm staring at the biggest jackass on the island," I told him.

There was a pause, a moment when everyone seemed to hold their breath after I had spoken, waiting to see what would happen next.

Then Kyle swung one fist, aiming at my head. I ducked and slammed my shoulder into his gut, knocking him into his friends, who all scrambled to leap on me in his defense. The punches came from every direction, slamming into my back, sides, head.

"Break it up!" a voice shouted over the noise. "Break it up now!"

Teachers ripped us apart, dragging each of us to different parts of the hall. Mr. Richter had hold of my left arm, his fingers digging painfully into my bicep. My lip pulsed, probably even more swollen than it had been before.

"Get to class!" Mr. Richter roared at the other students, who all scrambled away. Then he looked between those of us that were left. Kyle already had the purple bruise of what would probably become a black eye.

"You know the rules," Mr. Richter barked. "Suspension. All of you. You can explain it in my office while I call your parents."

Mr. Richter and the other teachers led us down the hall toward the guidance office. Kyle and his friends protested, but I tuned them out. It didn't matter. Nothing had ever mattered around here.

Chapter 13

I knew she would be there before I'd even broken through the trees to the little strip of beach, so I wasn't surprised to see the figure standing at the edge of the water.

"You're supposed to be at school," I said. It was the day of my suspension, the day after my fight with Kyle in the hall at school. My parents had given me strict instructions to stay at home all day while they were at work, but I was restless and had to get out of the house.

Elizabeth turned to me. The wind whipped her hair around her head, but I could tell she had been crying. Red lines etched across her eyes and on her nose.

"I'm sorry," she said, her voice cracking.

I stepped past her, barely dipping my toes into the surf where it slipped onto the wet sand. The ocean stretched out far to the horizon, empty and gray. Thick clouds hung in the sky and thunder rumbled over the water, but the storm was still far out to sea. If we were lucky, it would pass by without noticing the tiny island. Just like everything else did now, except the mists. They were still here, coating us like a blanket.

"Dylan." Elizabeth slipped her arms around my waist from behind, pressing her forehead into my shoulder blade. Her breath tickled my arm, sending a shiver through me. "Please talk to me."

"What are you sorry about?" I asked.

"About Kyle," she said. "And the other day. I'm sorry we fought."

"But you're not sorry about using me."

She lifted her head. "I told you, my daddy wants to leave the island. I have to do something."

There were two Elizabeths, and I could never be sure which one I was speaking to.

But there were also two Dylans. The water at my feet called to me, filling me with the strength of that other Dylan. The island was dying, we all knew that. Maybe there was some truth to the idea that it was being forgotten, as ridiculous as that might be. Maybe we would all be forgotten, those of us still stuck here.

But Elizabeth had a choice I didn't. She didn't have to be forgotten.

"You don't belong here," I said.

"This is my home."

I shook my head, pulling her arms away from me. "This island doesn't belong to you. The finfolk have been here a lot longer than your family has. It's *our* island and we'll run you off if we have to."

Elizabeth's mouth dropped open and she stepped

back. "We live here too."

"Do you know how your people have tormented us over the years?" I pointed at the bruises on my face. "Do you see what you've done? This island isn't yours anymore. We're done trying to live with you."

Elizabeth glared at me. "You're not the Dylan I know."

I shrugged, turning my back on her. "You never really knew me, did you? It was always a game, for both of us. I had my fun. I'm done with you now."

I knew my words had stung her, even though I kept my eyes on the horizon. I had to make her leave. I had to let her go, to let her have the chance I didn't.

"Fine," Elizabeth said after a moment. "If that's the way you want it to be."

"It is."

A moment passed, then I heard her footsteps crunch across the sand toward the path that would lead her back through the trees.

I closed my eyes, fighting back the urges inside me. One half told me to dive into the water and swim as far and as deep as I could.

The other half told me to run down that path leading into the trees.

But I didn't do either. I stayed where I was, trying to resist the calls of both land and water that fought inside me. I stood there, unmoving for a long time, watching the waves crash on the shore.

A crunch of sand and seashells behind me announced another presence some time later.

"So you want to tell me what's been going on?" Mara asked.

I watched a seagull dive toward the water, then swoop back toward the clouds. "Not really."

"Okay." Mara wrapped her arms around herself, lifting her face to the wind over the water.

I dug my hands into my pockets, hunching my shoulders in on myself. Foam gathered around my feet, the water licking at my ankles.

"How much longer do you think it'll take?" I asked.

I wasn't sure what I meant: how much longer before Josh and Sailor returned, or how much longer before we really did die out along with the island.

"I don't know," Mara answered.

"What should we do now?"

"We keep holding on, like we always do," Mara said.

* * *

"I think that's enough," Mr. Moody said as he took the broom from me. "You've been here all day, working yourself to death. You're going to be late."

"I can help you close," I said.

But Mr. Moody shook his head. "You don't belong here tonight, you know that."

I felt the pull inside me, calling me. It had grown stronger as the afternoon passed and night began to settle over the island. I knew it would be unbearable if I didn't go, but I wasn't sure Mr. Moody was right. I didn't know where I belonged anymore.

"Go on," Mr. Moody said. "Things are taken care of. I'll finish up."

I nodded and shoved my hands deep into my pockets. My old flip flops shuffled across the floor that was always sandy, no matter how much I swept it. Just as I reached the door, Mr. Moody cleared his throat.

"Do you..." He coughed and swept the broom back and forth over the floor at his feet. "Have you heard anything from Sailor?"

I had never heard him ask about Sailor before. She told me once that Mr. Moody had never really been a part of her life. He was her grandfather, and for reasons I didn't understand, he and Miss Gale had never married. I didn't know what the status of their relationship was these days, other than him being Miss Gale's employer. They never behaved any differently toward each other besides a neutral business relationship. Not that I'd seen anyway.

"No," I said. "I'm sorry. I haven't heard anything."

Mr. Moody continued sweeping the floor I had just swept and nodded, his gaze locked on the end of his broom. "Okay. Well, good night."

The night was black when I stepped outside the store. Fog hung thick in the air, and the wind blew leaves and bits of trash across the deserted street. Farther down the road, some of the homes glowed with light that shone through the windows. But not all of the homes were occupied that night.

I climbed onto my bike and followed the road toward the southern end of the island. There was no moon to light the street and I couldn't see more than a couple of feet in front of me, but I knew the way. Something inside pulled me along the road, closer to the beach where the rest of the people like me were gathered.

The crowd was restless when I arrived. Mom spotted me and waved, but I didn't go to join my family. My gaze scanned over the group, trying to count those who remained. Maybe thirty or so. I could remember Song Nights as a kid when the beach was full of finfolk waiting to swim and sing.

"I was starting to think you weren't coming," Mara said when she found me.

"I almost didn't."

My words hung in the air between us as we watched some little kids chase each other around the beach, laughing and shrieking.

"Do you regret not going with Sailor?" Mara asked.

I shook my head. "I don't want to be reminded how much different I am than everyone else. I don't want to see the homeland."

Mara crossed her arms, shivering in the cool wind that whipped around us. "Sometimes I wish I had gone. I wonder what it's like."

"Our ancestors came here to get away from it," I said. "Maybe there's a reason they decided to live among humans."

Mara shook her head. "You always talk about humans as if they're completely different from you. I've lived a human life, Dylan, and I can tell you, we're not that different."

The moment arrived. People began stripping off clothes, tossing them onto the beach behind them as they walked into the crashing surf at Pirate's Cove. One by one they disappeared into the blackness of the mists and water.

"We're different enough," I told her. "And around here, that's what matters."

I resisted the urge that vibrated inside me. My body

trembled and ached, but I wouldn't give in. I had come to a conclusion as I stood watching the others. Maybe I couldn't change what I was, but I could choose what form I wanted to be.

Mara paused as she unbuttoned her shorts. "You coming in?" she asked.

I studied the people like me, the ones who had never tried to fight for something different, who accepted life on the island as it was. But Elizabeth had shown me there was a different way. Maybe not now, but maybe someday, for those of us who chose to take it.

I didn't want to be stuck. I didn't want to be forgotten.

The ocean called to me, but I gritted my teeth together until my jaw ached. "No," I said softly. "I'm not."

Without waiting to see her reaction, I turned and walked back across the sand, burying the other Dylan deep inside.

About the Author

Most days, Shana Norris still feels like she's stuck at sixteen, which is probably why she enjoys writing about teens. She always wanted to be a mermaid and fell in love with the Outer Banks during a gray late winter years ago. She lives in a small town in eastern North Carolina with her husband and small zoo of pets, which currently includes two dogs, five cats, and five chickens.

Look for *Surrendering*, the final book in the Swans Landing series, coming Summer 2013.

To learn more about Swans Landing and the people living there, please visit www.shananorris.com.

Other books by Shana Norris:
The Boyfriend Thief
Troy High
Surfacing (Swans Landing Book 1)
Submerging (Swans Landing Book 2)
Something to Blog About

Swans Landing Series

Don't miss the rest of the books about the finfolk of Swans Landing!

Along the Outer Banks of North Carolina lies a small island that holds secrets as big as the ocean. A race of beings called finfolk walk among the humans, only changing into their mermaid form while swimming. For centuries, the humans and finfolk happily shared the island and the surrounding waters.

But that has changed.

Surfacing (Swans Landing #1)
Sixteen-year-old Mara Westray has just lost her mother, and now, being shipped off to live with the father she doesn't know is not how she imagined grieving. But from the moment she steps off the ferry, nothing is as ordinary as it looks.

Submerging (Swans Landing #2)
Sixteen years ago, Sailor Mooring's mother dove into the Atlantic Ocean and was never seen again. Now, Sailor is following her mother's long swim to find answers to the questions that have haunted her life: Why did her mother leave? And what really happened the night Sailor's father died?

Shifting (Swans Landing #3)
Dylan Waverly has lived his entire life on the tiny island of Swans Landing with his best friend Sailor Mooring at his side. But now Sailor has left, and no one knows if she'll ever return. Dylan remains stuck in a half-life between land and sea on an island that is slowly dying.

Surrendering (Swans Landing #4)
Josh Canavan swam an entire ocean in search of the truth about what happened the night his father died. Now he's made the journey back in order to save the people and the island he loves.

www.ingramcontent.com/pod-product-compliance
Lightning Source LLC
Chambersburg PA
CBHW070504130626
46555CB00003B/1153